Washita

WASHITA

McCain Cronicles
Book Seven

B.N. Rundell

WOLFPACK
PUBLISHING
— EST 2013 —

Washita
Paperback Edition
Copyright © 2023 B.N. Rundell

Wolfpack Publishing
701 S. Howard Ave. 106-324
Tampa, Florida 33609

wolfpackpublishing.com

Paperback ISBN 978-1-63977-196-7
eBook ISBN 978-1-63977-195-0
LCCN 2023951069

DEDICATION

In these past few days, I've been reminded about the brevity of time. The Bible says *The days of our years are threescore years and ten; and if by reason of strength they be fourscore years, yet is their strength labour and sorrow; for it is soon cut off, and we fly away.* Every day that passes makes each subsequent day all the more precious. I have passed the threescore years and ten and am rapidly approaching the fourscore. But God has blessed with each new day and my prayer is that someone reading these words will take heed, appreciate each new day, value it, use it not just for yourself but also for others, and have a great life. That's what I try to give my characters and by transposition to my readers all. Thank you for taking the time out of your life and use those precious moments to spend time together. You are appreciated!

WASHITA

CHAPTER 1

TRAIN

The clackety-clack of the wheels on the tracks had become a monotonous but tolerable background noise of the passenger car on the Union Pacific railway that pulled out of the station of Kansas City, Kansas. With no pullman car, Elijah McCain had taken a seat near the rear of the car and plopped the parfleche on the seat beside him. He removed his wide-brimmed felt hat and sat it atop the parfleche, ran his fingers through his hair and looked around at his fellow passengers. Most were men, but there were three women, one matronly-looking older woman sat beside her mousy looking man who she continually scolded and berated for everything from his appearance to his manner and lack of strength. Eli chuckled as he watched the repartee of the two, shaking his head as he considered the man who obviously had a very miserable life ahead.

The other two women were without a man, although one had a juvenile boy of about fourteen, rather gangly with a mop of blonde hair, who accompanied her, although she did not look old enough to be his mother. The other woman was alone and quite attractive with cascading red curls that fell over her shoulders and freckles that marched across her nose and cheeks. With curves in all the right places and a silk brocade dress in pale pink and yellow stripes, she appeared to be over-dressed in such unusual attire that was not common among traveling women. The single woman was seated opposite Eli and as he glanced her direction, he caught her looking his way, and nodded, to which she immediately turned to look out the window of the car.

Eli turned to look at the endless flats passing by the window and let his mind wander over the past few years since he was discharged from the Union Army at the rank of lieutenant colonel having served under General Sheridan through the last battle at Appomattox Court-house where the Confederacy surrendered to end the war. He returned to the home of his wife's family in Louisville, Kentucky to find his wife, Margaret, on her deathbed. She elicited a promise from him to find her boys, twin sons Jubal and Joshua, who had joined the Union army and deserted, choosing to find adventure in the western gold fields instead of fighting in the last days of the Civil War.

The covenant he made with his wife just before she died, sent him on a more than a year's long journey through the western lands in search of his stepsons. A journey that ended when he found his boys in Monterey, California, pursuing two sisters who had caught their attention aboard the Flying Cloud Clipper ship where the two were serving as shanghaied sailors. After they established their intentions with the girls, Eli and his sons, together with many recruited drovers, took a herd of a thousand remount horses from California across the western lands to Fort Hays, Kansas to General Sheridan. After delivering the horses, Eli and the boys continued on to Louisville where the girls and their mother were waiting and planning the nuptials.

It was when they met with Sheridan that the general had enticed Eli with the offer of continued service, not as a cavalry officer, but as a scout for the Indian fighting cavalry units out of Fort Hays. With his promise fulfilled to his wife, his future was a bit uncertain and the possibility of staying on the horse farm with his boys held little appeal, not after wandering for most of his career, with the exception of the years in the war, in the mountains of the west. He, like many a man that had seen the mountains and experienced the life of the wanderer, could not picture himself settled in a farmhouse in the woods of the flatlands. As he considered the offer from Sheridan, he decided to accept, and it was because of that acceptance that he was now traveling by train to the fort to meet with General Sheridan.

The train had a baggage car, two passenger cars, two stock cars, and a caboose. Never without his constant companions, his two horses were in the first of the stock cars. Rusty, his big claybank stallion, sometimes called a line-back red dun, and Grey, the dapple-grey mustang that served as his pack horse, although he had been Eli's primary mount when he served at Fort Laramie before the war. The rest of his gear was stacked in the same stock car, his saddle, bags, bedroll, pack saddle and panniers, and other supplies and his Spencer rifle and Colt revolver shotgun. He always had his Colt Army .44 in the holster on his left hip, butt forward and hidden behind his back, the LeMat nine-shot .42 revolver with the secondary center barrel that held a .20-gauge shotgun load with buckshot. Standing in the corner by

the parfleche was his Winchester Yellow-Boy lever action
.44 rifle. He also carried a sheathed Bowie knife that
hung out of sight between his shoulder blades at his
back.

The rattle and clatter of the coach blended with the
whine of wheels on the rails and the racketing of the
joining of the tracks as the big iron wheels rolled over
the joints. The creak and groan of the twisting and
jostling coach blended with the constant rattling of the
big wheels crossing the joints of the rails. The sounds
began to blend into a mesmerizing tone, and eyelids
grew heavy, but Eli fought against the drowsiness, and
reached for his parfleche and flipped open the flap, but
his attention was taken by the conductor who spoke as
he passed through. "Comin' up to Topeka! We'll have a
twenty-minute stop for all that wanna get sumpin' to
eat! Twenty minutes, and we wait for no one!"

Eli shook his head, but he had come prepared. With
the start of his train journey in Louisville, he made it a
point to keep his parfleche handy and full of foodstuffs.
The idea of rushing from the train to find something to
eat and downing it in a rush to get back was something
he had prepared against. Yet he knew many of the train
travelers were not as well prepared and he looked across
the aisle to see a consternated woman who looked back
and asked, "Twenty minutes? To get something to eat? Is
that possible?"

Eli grinned. "Some do it, but most either do without
or bring something. Which is what I've done. This is not
my first time so I had the cook at the hotel back at
Kansas City prepare me some vittles"—he nodded to his
parfleche—"so I wouldn't have to fight the crowd." He
paused, looked at the woman, and added, "Be happy to
share if you'd like. I've a good selection and I doubt if I

could eat it all before the end of my ride." He paused, lifted the lid on the parfleche and began to rummage around, looked back at the redhead and said, "Join me?" nodding to the empty seat in front of him. Every other row of seats faced the rear of the coach making room for conversational seating.

"Well, I don't know…" she answered, showing just the proper amount of hesitation until Eli answered. "There's plenty and I'd like the company," waving a hand to the empty seat.

She nodded and smiled. "Well, I am a bit hungry." She stood and moved across the aisle and joined him, facing him in the seat directly opposite. She was seated just as the train came to a stop and several of the passengers bustled to and fro to make their exit and get something to eat before the train pulled out again. As the train sat, huffing and puffing, letting off excess steam, the waterspout from the big tower lowered and the trough from the coal bin dropped as the train took on both water and coal. Although they had only come just over sixty miles, it would be a longer stretch until the next stop and they always topped off whenever possible.

"I'm Elijah McCain," began Eli, nodding to the redhead as she seated herself opposite. She smiled. "And I am Eleanor Whitcomb."

"Pleased to meet you. Is it Miss or Missus?"

She smiled coyly as she answered, "It is Miss Whitcomb, thank you."

"Pleased to meet you, Miss Whitcomb," responded Eli with a broad smile.

"Elly, or Eleanor, if you please, Elijah."

"Then by all means, call me Eli," answered Eli. He looked into the parfleche. "So, we have buttermilk biscuits and sausage, cornbread biscuits, a loaf of fresh baked bread, slices of roast beef, a few pieces of fried chicken, some pickles and a couple tomatoes that need slicing, and some apples. So, what would you like, Elly?"

"My, what an assortment, uh, maybe a slice of roast beef and a slice of that bread would suit me just fine, oh, and a pickle would be nice."

Eli chuckled and began digging through the treasure trove of goodies and produced a linen napkin and held the partially unwrapped package of beef for her to choose her slice and she looked from the meat to him with a question written on her face hesitating to reach, until Eli assured her, "Just pretend we're on a picnic and use the utensils God gave you," he held his fingers up and moved them to emphasize his words, smiling.

She smiled and chose a piece of meat, lay it on the napkin and watched as he brought out the loaf of bread, lifted his Bowie knife from the sheath at his back, much to the wide-eyed stare of his dinner companion, and began slicing off a couple pieces for the two of them. In short order, they had their laps full of food on their napkins and were doing their best to make it all disappear when several of the other passengers began filing back into the car to take their seats, and those that passed the two of them nodded and often commented, "I wish I'da thought of that."

With a long shriek of the train's whistle, the wheels began to turn, and the train pulled away from the station. As the conductor passed their seats, Elly asked, "How long until the next stop?"

"Depends on if'n any have flags out to stop us an' take on more passengers. If there ain't no flags, the next scheduled stop is Junction City, little more'n three hours."

"Thank you, sir," replied Elly with a smile. She turned

to Eli. "That would mean we would have time for a snack, don't you think?"

Again with a smile and a twinkle of mischief in her eyes. Eli guessed her to be midtwenties in age, but much more mature and confident than the typical young woman of the time. But he was not looking for a woman of any age, he'd had enough opportunities since his wife died, and he was not interested in the life of a married man. He still had too much wanderlust in his heart. The mountains had more of a draw than women. He stashed the remnants of their meal in the parfleche and set it aside, lifting his eyes to the vast distances of the rolling prairie land where the bluestem grasses waved in the breeze. He saw heavy black clouds gathering and knew they would be in for a storm but was confident the train would not be adversely affected.

He heard the screech of brakes as the train began to slow, yet it did not stop. The front door of the passenger car slammed open, and a whiskery-faced leering man stood before them with a pistol waving side to side as another man came behind him. "This hyar's a holdup! Now, you folks just put yore pokes and money in the bag hyar, an' ain't nuthin' gonna happen. The rest o' muh boys are emptyin' the safe in the baggage car an' soon's they're done, we'll be gone! So, like yo' momma used to say, just mind yore manners an' do as yore tol', unnerstan'?"

CHAPTER 2

CHASE

"Wal, what have we here?" questioned a leering outlaw, lustfully glaring at Elly and leaning against the side of the upright seat where she sat.

She turned slightly and looked up at the outlaw as his partner said, "Charlie, we ain't got time for that, you 'member what Frank said, 'git it and git out' now come on!"

"I ain't worried 'bout Frank an' if'n I wanna look o'er the merchandise, I'm gonna!" growled Charlie, glancing to his partner. "So, Simeon, you go on an' tell that brother o' your'n I'll be along directly." He chuckled. "An' I might be bringin' us some comp'ny to keep us warm tonight!" He cackled as he leaned down to grab Elly by her wrist and jerk her up out of her seat. Eli jumped to his feet but was met by the barrel of Charlie's pistol and a growl that said, "You wanna do sumpin' pilgrim?" He snarled as he pulled Elly close to him, using her as a shield as he backed down the center aisle, waving his pistol side to side. "Don't nobody do nuthin' or I'll crack her head open and shoot anyone what tries anythin'!" he growled, dragging Elly with him, his arm around her middle pinning her arms to her side.

Eli's hand dropped to the butt of his pistol, but Charlie watched him, snarling, with a look that dared Eli to try. Eli gritted his teeth, anger flaring his nostrils as he took a step toward the pair, but Charlie shot into the floor just inches from Eli's foot.

"Next one'll be 'tween yore eyes!"

He kicked the door aside and dragged Elly out with him. The train was screeching to a stop and the outlaws climbed down, arms full of plunder. Three men had hit the baggage car, and each carried a leather satchel, presumably full of money. One man had the horses on a long lead, and Charlie and Simeon had taken valuables from the passengers. Within moments, the six men were mounted and high tailing it away from the train, cutting a trail into the woods to disappear.

The conductor, followed by the brakeman, came into the passenger car to check on the passengers. He looked at Eli who still stood, although bent over a seat to look where the outlaws had gone, seeing Elly riding double with the man called Charlie. Eli stood up, turned to face the conductor.

"Anybody going to do anything?"

The conductor frowned at Eli. "We are, we're checkin' the passengers to see if everbody's alright. We had one man knocked out in the other car, but so far, that's all. You hurt or sumpin'?" he asked.

"NO! I'm talkin' about them," he said, motioning to the disappearing outlaws.

The conductor rose up and glared at Eli. "Now, just what would you have me do? Run 'em down by foot? Don't you know that's the Reno Brothers? They been robbin' trains from Indiana to Iowa, and now here! They just robbed a couple towns in Iowa an' the Pinkertons arrested 'em, put 'em in jail in Council Bluffs, but they escaped and now this. So what would you have me do? I'm just one man afoot," he declared, hands on hips as he pushed his rather abundant middle forward as if it would be used as a battering ram.

"Have they ever taken hostages before?" asked Eli.

"Dunno, don't think so, but they robbed several trains, county treasuries, banks, just about any place with money. Ain't never heard 'bout no hostages."

Eli nodded, glared at the brakeman, and said, "I've got horses in the stock car. I'm takin' 'em out, so keep this train stopped until I'm free, got it?"

"You goin' after 'em?" asked the brakeman.

"Somebody's gotta do somethin' and I can't just sit back and let them have that young lady."

"Yessir, I'll give you a hand with the ramp on the stockcar," answered the brakeman, sidestepping past Eli and heading to the door.

Eli gathered up his gear in the other seat, and with arms full, he followed the brakeman. The man was sliding open the wide door when Eli dropped his armload of gear on the ground, stepped to the side of the door and helped the brakeman lower the ramp. He stepped up and went into the car to quickly saddle his claybank stallion, Rusty, then gear up his pack horse, Grey, and led both animals down the ramp. After helping the brakeman replace the ramp and slide the big door closed, Eli tightened cinches, stepped aboard Rusty and with a wave to the brakeman, started off at a trot to round the back of the train's caboose and cross the tracks to get on the trail of the outlaws. Before he crossed the meadow of tall grass, he heard the train sound its whistle, and start the chug, chug, chugging to pull away.

———

"NOW YOU'VE DONE IT! What're we gonna do with a woman?!" barked Frank Reno, the recognized sole leader of the gang since his brother, John, was arrested after their holdup of the Daviess County Courthouse in Gallatin, Missouri, and sentenced to twenty-five years in the Missouri State Penitentiary. Frank looked from Charlie, who held the woman on the seat of the saddle before him, and to his own brother Simeon. He growled at his brother, "Simeon! You should know better than to take a woman! The railroad and the townsfolks will be up in arms! It's bad 'nuff when we get their money, but now, one of their women?" He shook his head, nudged his mount closer to Charlie's and looked at the woman. "What's your name?"

"Eleanor Whitcomb."

"Your man on the train?"

"No. I was traveling alone, but I'm meeting my *man* in Junction City. We're to be married there."

Frank looked her up and down, noticing the expensive-looking dress and the reticule she held tightly before her. "What's your man do?"

Eleanor glared at the outlaw, her nostrils flaring. "He's the banker! He is a very influential man in the town and when he hears about this, he'll have the whole town after you!"

"Lady, you've got me plumb scared! Why, can't you see I'm just shakin' in my boots?!" He laughed, shook his head, then grew serious. "Banker, huh? He just work there or is he the owner or manager or what?"

Eleanor lifted her chin in defiance. "He owns the bank!"

"Hmmm, maybe we *can* do something with this." He showed a face of anger as he looked at Charlie. "You keep your hands off her and if she so much as tears that dress, I'll take it outta your hide!" He turned back to Eleanor. "We're gonna make camp up here a ways, an' then you'll be writin' your banker friend a little note and if'n he does what I tell him, you'll get cut loose an' no harm'll come to you. But if'n he don't…" He shrugged, grinning, and nudged his mount away. With a wave of his hand, he motioned the men to follow, and he took a dim trail through the thick trees.

———

ELI HAD JUST ENTERED the thicket of towering oaks and hickory with cottonwoods and hackberry intermixed, when the dark clouds that had been hovering low overhead let loose. The thunder rumbled, jagged swords of lightning stabbed at the trees and rain began to pelt the leafy canopy. Eli stopped, stepped down, grabbed his slicker from his bedroll and slipped it on. It was a long rubberized Mackintosh style that was split in the back so it would fall on either side of the saddle. His felt hat was wide brimmed and offered ample protection for his head. He stepped back aboard Rusty and started him and Grey off at a trot, and when he broke from the trees, a wide meadow like clearing showed the obvious trail of the outlaws and he kicked the stallion up to a lope. He knew he had to get as close as possible before the rain obliterated the trail, but he was confident he could follow that big a bunch for they would leave an obvious trail, even in the mud and tall grass.

The rain was steady, just a good rain for the farmer's crops, without a lot of wind and nothing extraordinarily heavy. Eli grinned as he watched the trail before him, it reminded him of the parting of the red sea told about in scriptures where Moses led the children of Israel to freedom, the tall bluestem grass laid aside by the passing of six horses evidently not riding in a single file, but at least two and three abreast, making tracking that much easier. He lifted his eyes to the sky, and the rain appeared to be lessening or at least moving on to the west and he guessed there would be about three, maybe four more hours of daylight. According to the trail, the band of outlaws was not slowing, and he guessed they probably had their night's camp already chosen and they were bound for that spot. Exactly what he would be able to do could only be determined after he found their camp and located Elly, but he knew he would have to do something.

Chapter 3

Plan

Another hour and the rain began to let up, becoming little more than a pesky drizzle. A quick glance to the sky showed sunshine pushing through the tail end of the storm clouds and long lances of bright sunlight began to chase even the drizzle away. Eli slowed, stripped off the mackintosh and tied it behind the cantle of his saddle, stood in his stirrups and searched for a high point to get a better look at the lay of the land. The trail of the outlaws bore northeast, and Eli was certain they had already determined where they would be making camp. He hoped to get them spotted before dusk so he could formulate a plan to get Elly out of their clutches.

He pulled the binoculars from their case in the saddlebags and lifted them for a better search. Directly in line with the trail of the highwaymen rose a cluster of timber covered hills, none more than seventy or eighty feet higher than the flat rolling terrain of the land, but certainly inviting for someone wanting to find a hidden camp for the night. His only reservation was they were only about twenty to thirty miles from the holdup and most outlaws want to put as much distance between them and the location of the robbery as possible, but that was usually for fear of pursuit by a posse, but with no nearby town, and no lawmen on the train, maybe they were not concerned about immediate pursuit.

Rather than continue on their trail, Eli chose to risk losing them by swinging wide of the grassy meadow, keep to the trees and make for the highest point of the distant hills that he thought would be the location of their camp, at least for this one night. He pushed on, crossed a two-track trail or road that was probably some farmer's road to his home place for it had seen little travel and that by the wide wheels of a farm wagon. Beyond the road, he hugged the tree line, and used the open edges of a bluestem grass meadow to make the way for his horses a bit easier and more direct. As he neared the highest butte, he pushed into the trees and stopped at the first partial clearing. He stopped, waited and listened, and with nothing more than the scolding chatter of a squirrel, Eli stepped down and with Spencer and binoculars in hand, started to make his way to the crest of the hill.

Once atop the knoll, he found a bit of an opening and stood under the wide stretching limbs of a big bur oak. Before he lifted the binoculars, he smelled woodsmoke, grinned and dropped to his haunches to take his time to search below for the camp of the outlaws. Twisting through the low hills and thick woods, a creek that he would later learn was Soldier Creek, pushed against the flanks of the hill where he sat, bent back on itself around a smaller knob of a hill, and meandered southward. He heard the sounds of breaking branches and knew someone was below him, probably breaking up some firewood. With a quick look around to determine the lay of the hill and any trails that cut through the woods, Eli began to pick his way closer to the low-lying camp.

He heard them before he saw them, and he bellied down to crawl closer, using the thicker underbrush of berry bushes and willows. He stopped when he heard the men talking, slowly pushed aside a handful of willows to see into their camp, wanting to see Elly and make sure she was at least temporarily safe. He heard one man, apparently the boss of the group, say, "Charlie, I'm sendin' you into Junction City with her message to her banker friend!"

"Me? Why me? I'm the one that got her!"

"That's why I'm sendin' you, we all know how you are with women, and I don't want her touched!"

"But Frank, that's two, three days from here!" whined the big man, looking from Frank Reno to the woman and back.

"Then you better get started!"

"Now? Muh horse is tired an' I'm hungry!"

"Then at first light, and if you keep movin' you might make it in less time!"

Eli watched as Charlie grumbled, kicking at the dirt and reached down, picked up a twig, broke it, and tossed the pieces into the trees, almost hitting the brush in front of Eli.

Frank turned to the other men. "Simeon, you and William take care of that woman. Make her comfortable and get her started writing that note to her banker friend. William, you make sure nobody touches her and that includes you!"

"What'chu want her to write, Frank?" asked Simeon.

"That she's safe and will be returned for ten thousand

dollars cash! He has till the end of the week to deliver the money."

"Where to?"

Frank frowned, sat down and thought, then lifted his head. "At the Pottawatomie Indian Pay Station, at the edge of Saint Mary's!"

"Why the Indian pay station?"

"It's near that church and they won't want anything happenin' there!"

Once that was decided, Frank ordered the others to tend to the horses, picket them nearby and stack the gear. "We'll be here a few days so let's get comfortable," he declared, standing with hands on his hips as he looked around at their temporary home. He looked at the woman. "Can you cook?" he growled.

"Yes, I can cook!" declared the obstinate Elly, sitting with arms crossed before her.

"Then make yourself useful!" He motioned to the packs beside the cookfire. "Everything you need's in them packs. Coffee, beans, cornmeal, meat. So fix us somethin' good. I been missin' a woman's cookin!"

Eli grinned to himself, and began searching the area, looking for any vulnerabilities. It was a good camp, formed eons ago by the continue washing of the creek against the clay and rocky soil of the hill, cutting into the hip of the hill, and making a well-protected wide bank with a rocky overhang that gave added protection from above. With ample room for the horses, if need be, it had room for all the men and their bedrolls, packs and more. With the creek making a wide horseshoe bend around the point of the lower hill opposite their camp, it was well hidden from any of the flats that surrounded the area.

But as Eli searched the area, an idea began to form.

With the setting sun stretching long shadows, those same shadows also pointed to a rocky escarpment opposite the camp, there were trees that had taken root in the crevices of the stony face that would also offer what Eli needed. He grinned and began pushing his way back from the shrubs and undergrowth, and when clear, he slowly stood, and carefully picked his way back to the tethered horses, his plan taking shape as he moved.

There was a trickle of water near the small clearing and he led the horses for a drink, let them crop a little grass, and returned to the clearing to strip the animals of their gear. With the horses picketed, he adjusted the sling on the Spencer and hung it over one shoulder, then with the Winchester Yellow Boy in hand, he went through the trees to cross Soldier Creek on the back side of the butte, out of sight from the men in the camp. Once across, he turned to the lower timber covered butte with the rocky escarpment and worked his way quietly through the trees in the fading light of dusk. As he neared the rocky shoulder, he paused, searched the sky for the first stars to light their lanterns, looked for the moon that was waxing full, and with a thorough search of the camp on the far side of the creek, he worked his way to the trees on the escarpment.

When he crossed the creek, he soaked a handful of rawhide strips, and now withdrew them from the pouch and began his work. He picked the small red oak, and placed the Winchester, tying it in place with two strips of rawhide, carefully positioning the rifle so it was aimed at the tree that held one end of the picket line for the horses. He had jacked a round into the chamber before positioning the rifle and now, carefully and slowly tied a strip of wet rawhide to pull the trigger back as far as possible without dropping the hammer. He tied it tight, wiped off any excess water, and stepped back away from the tree. He turned to face the east and made certain the rising sun would have unrestricted access to the wet rawhide. He was counting on the sun to finish the job.

He moved to a mature hackberry tree on the far side of the escarpment and repeated his action with the Spencer rifle. He checked again that it had unrestricted view of the rising sun, carefully tied back the trigger as far as possible so that the slightest tightening on the drying rawhide would drop the hammer, checked the other strips to ensure the rifle was aimed dead center of the cook fire and stepped away.

He chuckled and muttered a short prayer. "Lord, please make sure that Elly is not by the cookfire when that Spencer fires." He was planning on the woman making an early breakfast and being away from the fire before the rising sun dried and shrunk the rawhide to pull the trigger.

CHAPTER 4

SURROUNDED

E li sat on a rock near the horses, his eyes on the first grey light of early morning. The sky was void of any clouds and the eastern horizon glowed pink from north to south, a color that faded to the dusty blue and distant darkness as the slow rising sun gave chase to the retreating night sky. Eli knew it would be a while before the direct sunlight could begin its work on the rawhide and he shrugged as he flipped open the Bible, he held in his lap. He shuffled the pages until he stopped at the beginning of the book of Psalms and began to read, *Blessed is the man that walketh not in the counsel of the ungodly, nor standeth in the way of sinners, nor sitteth in the seat of the scornful. But his delight is in the law of the Lord; and in his law doth he meditate day and night.* He lifted his eyes to the east, thought for a moment about his plan, and sought the face of the Lord as he continued to read, *And he shall be like a tree planted by the rivers of water...* He chuckled as he pictured the trees that would be his allies and continued, *that bringeth forth his fruit in his season; his leaf also shall not wither; and whatsoever he doeth shall prosper. The ungodly are not so but are like the chaff which the wind driveth away. Therefore, the ungodly shall not stand in the judgment, nor sinners in the congregation of the righteous. For the Lord knoweth the way of the righteous: but the way of the ungodly shall perish.*

Eli grinned, slowly closed the Bible and lifted his eyes to the eastern sky and shrugged. "Lord, we've got 'em surrounded, now let's just hope they see things our way. We need to deliver Elly from the ungodly, so…" He stood, swapped the Bible for the Colt revolving shotgun and started to the crest of the hill.

As he topped out on the hill, he stepped under the big bur oak and searched the surrounding area for any last-minute surprises, but there was nothing, save a pair of white-tailed bucks taking water at the edge of the creek upstream of the camp. The deer took their drink and leisurely walked away from the creek to find their morning breakfast in the flats.

With shotgun in hand, Eli cautiously and quietly made his way through the trees, careful to watch every step. In hardwood forests, although the ground is covered with fallen leaves and offered quiet passage, those same leaves could be hiding brittle broken branches that if stepped on, the breaking of the branch in the quiet of the woods could sound as loud as a pistol shot. He felt his way, every step carefully placed only after feeling with his moccasin'd foot. He had learned the way of the natives when he was stationed at Fort Laramie and applied those lessons carefully.

The horses were picketed on the upstream side of the overhang, facing into the trees. Eli had chosen a place on the downstream side of the camp where a big black walnut tree that had withstood the years of high water and wearing away of the embankment and still stood strong, some of its roots stretching toward the low water creek. The big tree stood fifty to sixty feet tall, standing solitary guard on that point of the embankment with a trunk that was wider than the broad-shouldered Eli affording him good cover that no rifle bullet could penetrate.

A cluster of cottonwood saplings, underbrush of chokecherries offered cover and as he pushed past a thicket of blackberries, he could not resist grabbing a handful for his breakfast. He carefully and quietly chose a spot in the thicket where he would wait for the attack from his sunshine accomplices on the escarpment and seated himself to enjoy the blackberries. He was near enough, he could hear some of the conversations, but all that was heard was more complaining by Charlie about his ride to Junction City.

Frank stood before Charlie and growled, "I got to thinkin' 'bout you goin' all the way to Junction City an' I think it'd be better if you just go to Manhattan. There's a telegraph station there and you can send her friend a telegram instead. An' if you can figger out how to do it without them seein' yore face, all the better." He dug in his pocket, produced a pair of ten-dollar gold pieces and handed them to Charlie. "Now, lemme see that note an' I'll shorten it for the telegram."

Eli's attention was caught when the rising sun bent its long rays over the treetops and let the bright morning sunlight slide down the leafy tree cover to pierce the trees with lances of gold. Eli grinned as he looked across the way to the escarpment. He could not make out the rifles, but he recognized the chosen trees, and the warm sun was bathing those trees in bright sunlight. He grinned, stood and with the Colt shotgun before him, slowly picked his way toward the black walnut tree.

There was a short stretch between his cover and the tree that he would wait to cross until the first shot, then he could make his move when all eyes were on the far hillside.

Fifteen minutes, twenty, and the men in the camp were finishing their breakfast. Frank stood, looked at Elly who had retreated to the edge of the clearing where she had made her bed away from the men, and called out, "Hey woman! That was some good cookin'! Liked that cornbread…" And the big coffee pot that sat on the creek side of the cook fire exploded, the roar of the big Spencer echoed across the creek, the sound bouncing around the overhang and all the men dove for cover, only there was little cover to be had. Charlie had been begrudgingly saddling his horse when the Winchester blasted the tree near the picket line and all the horses spooked, jerked against the line tearing it free and as a disjointed team, the horses stampeded into the trees, kicking, grunting, snorting, and bucking.

The few rocks that had been piled up at the edge of the creek had become the breastworks for the gang as they lined out and hunkered down. "Where'd that come from?" shouted Simeon.

Frank hollered, "Where are they?"

"Who are they?" shouted the third brother, William.

With no answers coming, Charlie Anderson slowly lifted his head between two of the bigger rocks and looked across the creek. "I think they're up there by them rocks!" he declared.

But a voice came from behind them. "Nope, we're behind you!" declared Eli. Before they could turn, he added, "And I've got a ten-gauge shotgun covering you, so don't move unless you want a backside full of double-aught buck!"

Frank tried to turn his head to see who was behind them, but Eli growled, "I said don't move till I tell you! Now, throw your guns in the creek! NOW!" he shouted. The splashes of pistols hitting the water were clear. While they moved, Eli motioned to Elly to go back into the trees the way he had come. "Now, Charlie, you won't be needin' to take that trip Frank said, cause I'm takin' the woman with me! And just to show you there's no hard feelin's, I don't care about the money you took from the baggage car or anything else. If you remember Charlie, I'm the one that was with the woman when you came into the car and you forgot to get my poke, so I count myself lucky. Now, you fellas can just stand up and start walkin' after your horses, but first, take off your boots and throw them in the creek with your guns!"

"We can't do that! Not in our stockin' feet, we can't!" whined Charlie.

The others groaned and grumbled, but Eli said, "Either that or buckshot, which do you want, Charlie?" He chuckled.

Charlie whined, "An' the woman's gone!" He pointed, but Eli did not turn.

"Ummhmmm, I reckon she's had enough of the bunch of you. And if you're smart, you'll get after your horses, then maybe by the time you get back, your boots and guns will still be there and not wash too far downstream. Then you can load up your stuff and go back to the other side of the Mississippi where you have so many friends just waiting for you to come home!"

Six stocking-footed men traipsed across the corner of what had been their camp and took to the trail made by the stampeding horses. When they disappeared into the trees, Eli started to the creek, but the crack of a branch turned him back to where the men had gone to see Frank starting toward him. Eli lifted the shotgun and blasted the dirt in front of the man.

"I don't wanna hafta kill you, Frank, but I will! Now git!" He motioned with the shotgun and Frank turned and tiptoed through the trees to follow the others.

Eli walked to the creek bank, looked to see the boots and guns in the water, most of the boots floating with the current, chuckled and turned back to the trees and Elly. She was waiting just inside the trees, and they quickly mounted the shoulder of the hill to get to the horses. Quickly saddling up, he adjusted the packs, shared some of the load by tying it behind his saddle and made the packsaddle as comfortable as possible with his bedroll, lifted Elly aboard and led the way across the creek. He made short work of retrieving the two rifles, slipped the Spencer into the second scabbard, and chose to carry the Winchester across the pommel of his saddle, always at the ready. With the sun behind them and slightly off their left shoulder, they headed across the flats, bound for the railroad and the nearest town of Manhattan.

CHAPTER 5

RETURN

"That conductor showed me a map of this country, an' dependin' on where you wanna go, we could take a couple ways to get there," explained Eli. They were sitting in the shade of a big bur oak and watching the horses graze on the grass beside the little creek, as they had some jerky and waited on the coffee to perk a mite.

Elly looked at her rescuer, smiled, and answered, "I was on my way to Junction City to meet my intended, Humphrey Hogan. We were to be married..." She paused, turned to look at Eli. "But after that experience, I'm not sure he would still want to marry me..." She chuckled and continued, "And I'm not sure he's the man for me. He just, well, in the city, he was somebody special, you know, in the banking business, important, a little smug, and impressive. But out here when I compare what I remember of him and having met some...well some *real* men." She covered her mouth as she giggled and added, "I guess my father was right, he really is kind of a sissy britches!"

Eli could not help but laugh and turn to look at Elly. He shook his head. "Reckon it's good for you to realize that before you get hitched! What'd your father do, I mean, to make a living?"

"He was a career soldier, a doctor in the Union Army. Retired as a lieutenant colonel. So, you can understand why he said that about Humphrey."

"I can, and to most of the Army doctors I knew, most every man that wasn't in the war would be considered a sissy britches." Eli chuckled.

"But now, I don't know what to do!" she declared. "Should I go on to Junction City, or…" She shrugged.

"Do you have family back in Kansas City or somewhere else?"

"My father is there, my mother passed about a year ago, consumption."

"Any other prospects back there?" asked Eli.

Elly took a deep breath that lifted her shoulders as she reached for the coffeepot to pull it back from the flames and let the brew settle. "None that I knew. Humphrey was considered the best of the bunch."

"Well Elly," began Eli, reaching for the cups to pour the coffee. "We're headin' west. Next little town is Saint Mary's, after that is Manhattan, then Junction City. You can catch a train goin' either way from any of those towns. There's not much west of here, oh, the railroad is pushing west but the furthest west it is, is Cheyenne, Wyoming, and that's not much of a town. For us to make Junction City, we would cut across country, cross the Kansas River, and reach Junction City about sundown tomorrow. But if you'd rather catch a train back east sooner, we could go to Saint Mary's or Manhattan." He paused, poured the cups full of coffee and sat back on the log, elbows on his knees as he held the steaming cup in his hands and looked at Elly. "If we go on to Junction City, you might see Humphrey and decide to stay, or after you talk a little, you might want to return to Kansas City or…" He shrugged.

"Is there any way to go west beside the railroad?" queried a frowning but thoughtful Elly.

"'Bout the only way I know is to catch a stagecoach or join a wagon train of settlers."

"Would that be safe?"

"Was the railroad safe?" Eli chuckled, sipping his coffee.

Elly shook her head. "Then let's go to Junction City. I'll talk to Humphrey and then decide." She frowned and looked back to Eli. "Could I get a stage or wagon train from Junction City?"

"Probably. Fort Riley is there, and most wagon trains stop to resupply, and the stage goes through there."

She smiled, nodding, slipping into private thoughts, and sipped her coffee.

————

THEY HEADED SOUTHWEST, crossed the tracks and the Kansas River where Eli shot a pair of ducks for their supper and continued westerly, following a wagon road that pointed toward Junction City. By dusk, they dropped into a little swale with a meandering creek and a shallow pond with an abundance of water birds, frogs and more. They stripped the horses of the gear and after Eli laid out the pans and pots, Elly set about making supper with the ducks while Eli went searching for some eggs for their breakfast. He returned with a broad smile and a hat full of duck eggs and some cattail shoots to add to their supper.

When they sat back with full stomachs and a hot cup of coffee, Eli on the log, Elly on the ground using the log for a backrest, and they looked at the night sky, listening to the sounds of the night. The bullfrogs were providing a deep rumble to accompany the repeated honk of the loons, while the big-eyed owl asked his question of the night. A pair of coyotes, separated by the hills, sent their lonesome cry into the darkness, hoping for a connection, but the rattle of trace chains interrupted the reverie and Eli came to his feet, picked up the shotgun and walked to the edge of the camp, looking into the darkness and wondering what fool was driving a wagon in the darkness.

"Hello, the camp!" came a shout from the dark. "Saw your fire, need some help!"

The only sound that came from the voice was a low cry and the restless stomping of a team. Eli moved from the trees, the low burning fire glowing in the glen. "Who are you and whaddaya need?"

"I'm Nathan Billings, I'm a farmer an' muh wife's tryin' to birth a baby, but she's havin' trouble! We need some help if you can!" pleaded the man.

Eli stepped easily through the darkness, seeing the silhouette of the wagon and the man standing in front of the seat. Eli saw no weapon and moved to the rear of the wagon silently. He saw the blanket-covered figure, heard the moans of the woman, and spoke to the man, "I'm here. Pull the wagon closer to the camp. I've a woman there, maybe she can help."

"Oh, thank God," moaned the man, dropping onto the seat and slapping reins to the team. As they came into the dim light, Eli called out, "Elly! There's a woman here that's tryin' to birth a child. She needs your help!"

Elly jumped to her feet and came quickly to the

wagon, glanced to the man and Eli. "You need to get her by the fire, quick! I've helped with this before but each one is different." She turned to Eli. "Get some water on the fire and get some bandages, rags, something!" She looked at the man. "How long has she been like this?"

"It started 'bout midday, she tried on her own while I was in the field, but when I came in she was on the floor, bleedin' and such. I loaded her up right away, we ain't got no neighbors, no doctor, nuthin', so I was headin' to Junction City. That's all I knew to do!" he pleaded, shaking his head, his hands trembling with his fear.

"What's her name?"

"Mary, Mary Elizabeth."

Elly nodded and motioned to Nathan. "You go help Eli. I'll tend to her. My father was a doctor, and I helped him a few times, so…" She turned away, looking to the woman now lying on a blanket in the firelight.

"Mary, I'm Elly. I'm going to help you the best I can, but I need you to help me, alright?"

The woman, sweat beading on her brow, blood showing on the towels and more that lay beneath her, gritted her teeth, squinched her eyes tight and tried to nod. She let out a long breath, took another deep breath and tensed all over as Elly moved beside her knees and began to examine the woman.

———

IT WAS A RESTLESS NIGHT, even the horses were tense and edgy, Mary's screams pierced the darkness and Nathan paced nervously while Eli tended the fire and the pots of water. Eli glanced from Nathan to the women and back. He looked to the night sky to see the big moon that was waning from full as it hung lonesome in the dark sky. The night lanterns that hung beneath the few clouds did little to encourage the struggling women, and Elly stood, walked to Eli and glanced to Nathan.

She shook her head. "Is there any way we can keep going? This is more than I can handle. The baby is twisted around, it's what they call breech, and I can't get it straight. She needs a doctor."

Nathan had stepped close. "The closest doctor is in Junction City, that's where I was headed, but..." He shook his head and sobbed. "That's most of a day away."

"And I don't know if the ride would be too much for her, but I just don't know. She's lost so much blood, I'm afraid..." replied a pleading somber Elly, glancing from Eli to Nathan.

"Please ma'am, do what'chu can, she needs a woman close by now," asked Nathan, tears making muddy trails down his face. Elly nodded and turned back to the woman.

CHAPTER 6

CHANGE

The big farmer was pacing about, wringing his hands and mumbling prayers as he looked heavenward with an occasional glance to the woman whose shadow stretched to meet the darkness. The moan and cry of his wife pierced his soul, and he shook his head, dropped to his knees, and lifted his tear-streaked face to the night sky, pleading with God.

Elly called out, "You men! Come here!"

Both men jumped to their feet and came close to Elly as she looked up and began barking orders. "Nathan, you take one of those blankets and cut it into strips this wide"—holding her hands less than shoulder-width apart —"and get them wet in the cold water, wring them out a little but make sure they're good and wet, and get them here to me, NOW!" she barked.

Nathan nodded and turned to the stack of gear with their belongings from the wagon and began ripping the blankets.

Elly looked at Eli. "Eli, you do the same, but first, put some big flat rocks as near the fire as you can, we need them hot to heat the pieces of blanket you're going to get! Hurry!"

Both men were frowning, trying to think of what she might be doing, but neither could come up with an answer. Nathan was first to bring a stack of folded wet blankets to Elly and was surprised to see his wife uncovered, except for her shoulders and feet. He frowned but said nothing as he watched Elly start to unfold the blanket strips, wave them in the air to get them even colder, and lay one across his wife's belly, just below her breasts. As Elly worked, she continually encouraged Mary Elizabeth. Elly looked at Nathan. "Go! Get some more!" and watched as Nathan trotted off to the stack of gear to do as he was bidden.

Eli came close with a small stack of folded blankets, moving them from hand to hand because of the warmth. Elly grabbed the top blanket, unfolded and refolded it to a double thickness, twice the width she had directed, and laid the warm blanket across the lower portion of the woman's belly, covering the top of her thighs as well. Elly waved Eli away and he returned to the rocks by the fire to retrieve more blankets.

The relay of blankets continued for another hour or more and Elly waved both men away and began working on Mary Elizabeth, reaching to try to complete the turning of the baby. She knew that with a breech, it was important to get the baby turned to exit headfirst and the purpose of the cold and the warm blankets, was to try to encourage the baby to move away from the cold and go to the warmth. Elly felt and smiled, nodding, although the men were standing near the fire and had been directed to not watch.

The moon was resting on the western hills, anxious to tuck itself away for the night, and the eastern sky was beginning to blush pink, when the still of the morning was shattered by the wail of the newborn girl. Elly laid the child on Mary Elizabeth's lower chest as she began to cut the cord and tie it off. With the second breath, the baby lowered its squall to something just a little less than a norther thunderstorm, but the baby's daddy was on his knees beside his weary wife who lay listless, with sunken eyes, and forcing a smile as she lay one hand on the legs of the infant. Elly forced a tired smile as she nodded to the couple and accepted a hand from Eli to come to her feet.

Eli helped the midwife to the fire and the smooth grey log, handed her a cup of steaming coffee, poured one for himself, and sat down beside her. She leaned close to Eli, laid her head on his shoulder, and breathed a heavy sigh of relief. She stared at the flickering flames, whispered just loud enough for Eli to hear, "I don't think Mary Elizabeth will survive this day."

Eli sat quiet, knowing there was nothing he could say that would help at a time like this. Elly had become very invested with the mother and baby, and her heart was breaking for the woman. She sat up, sipped her coffee, took a deep breath that lifted her shoulders and looked over at Nathan who sat beside his wife, and reached to take the baby off her breast. As he held the infant, he looked over to Elly, wide-eyed and fear showing on his face. Elly came to her feet and went to the couple, smiled as she saw Mary grinning at her husband, but both showed themselves to be weary. Elly took the child, wrapped her tight, and asked, "Have you chosen a name for this little girl?" trying to be positive and happy for them.

Mary Elizabeth slowly nodded, forced a smile and

looked at Nathan who replied, "Matilda Letitia, after our"—nodding to his wife—"mothers."

Elly smiled. "Are either of the grandparents near?"

Nathan shook his head. "No, we have no one. 'Bout ten years ago, we came out west with our families with one of the early wagon trains, but it was hit by a band of Kiowa. Most were killed, but we"—nodding to his wife again—"and four others that were away picking berries, survived. We all stayed and worked together to build homes. None of us were more'n fifteen at the time, but we all made it."

Elly looked at Nathan who was a big man, broad-shouldered, a shock of red hair, and was about six feet tall. It was obvious he was a heavily muscled man by the way the buttons on his shirt pulled at the material every time he took a breath. He wore heavy denim overalls held up by broad galluses, hobnail boots and a homespun shirt. He had a rugged but somewhat handsome look about him, but that look was marred now by worry and dark fearful eyes. Elly looked from the big man to the frail woman and the tiny infant in her arms, slowly shaking her head with concern about both the woman and the infant. The man she saw that showed such tenderness to his wife and infant, also showed his ignorance about such things as taking care of a helpless child. He would do his best, but he had a farm to tend, animals to care for, and a helpless wife, and that was if she survived even this day.

Elly looked at Nathan. "Sit with her, hold her hand, but let her get some rest. I'll take the baby for a while, and it wouldn't hurt for you to get some rest also."

"Yes'm," answered Nathan, showing a grateful smile, but worry filled his eyes as he scooted a little closer to his woman.

Eli had made a bit of a bed for Elly, he had watched as she helped the couple and knew she would return with the baby, and as she neared, he motioned for her to lie down with the baby. "We still have a couple blankets we didn't cut up, so you make yourself and the baby comfortable. We'll just stay here another day and I'll take over cooking duties and maybe after the bunch of you get a little rest, I might have some stew or somethin' ready," he chuckled as she went down on one knee, then the other and gently lay down on the bedroll, cradling the baby in her arm and holding her tight. Eli pulled the blanket over the pair and with a nod, stepped away.

Mary Elizabeth struggled with taking any nourishment, which made it difficult to feed the baby, but she managed enough. As the day waned and dusk began to drop its curtain, Eli was at the cookfire stirring the hanging pot of beef stew made from the leftovers from his travel rations in the parfleche. The coffee pot was dancing on the rock and Elly was with the family and tending to the baby. The sudden wail lifted into the darkened sky, startling Eli, who turned with pistol in hand, but it was not a threat. Nathan had dropped to his knees, sobbing as he clung tightly to the hand of his tiny wife. Elly sat back on her heels, lifting the baby from her mother's bosom, and with a quick glance to Eli at the fire, he knew the life had slipped from Mary Elizabeth.

Eli sat back on the grey log, hanging his head with compassion for Nathan and the infant, knowing the days before them would be some of the most difficult in their lives. He glanced to Elly who stood, and started to the cookfire, leaving Nathan alone with the body of his wife. She sat beside Eli at the fire, tucked the blanket around the baby and told Eli the story of the families of the two and how they were all alone. She shook her head. "I don't know how he will manage; he knows nothing about a baby. And his grief…" She shrugged, shaking her head with sympathetic sorrow.

"Well, you need to keep your strength up, so I'll dish you up a plate of food and some coffee, then I'll hold the baby while you eat," offered Eli.

Elly grinned. "And just what do you know about babies?"

"I know they eat, make a mess, and eat some more. And in between times, they beller a lot!" He chuckled.

"So, that tells me you know absolutely nothing!" Elly grinned.

"I don't even know anything about 'em after they grow up!" mumbled Eli as he stepped to the cook pot with plate in hand and began dishing up her supper.

CHAPTER 7

SEPARATION

The gold letters on the frosted glass in the door read, *Humphrey A. Hogan, President.* Eli chuckled to himself as he sat back in the chair and hung his hat on the toe of his boot at his crossed legs. With his arms crossed on his chest, he looked around the spacious room that held two desks with side chairs, a wooden rail that separated the entry to the teller windows and the president's office. The squirrelly-looking clerk with sleeve garters and an eye shade had disappeared into the office and unintelligible words could be heard from within. The door opened and the clerk nodded, glanced around the room, and motioned for Eli to come near. In a low voice, the clerk said, "He's not happy, but he'll see you now," and motioned toward the door for Eli to enter.

As Eli opened the door, he saw a man of average height, a well-tailored pinstripe suit that did little to hide that ample paunch that pushed against the tight buttons of the waistcoat, and a scowling face that lay between thick mutton chop sideburns that joined the whiskery lip of the man. His nostrils flared as he stood behind his desk and glared at Eli and growled. "Now what is it that's so important you couldn't wait? Come on, I don't have much time, out with it!" he demanded.

Eli gave a half-smile, half-smirk of an expression as he casually seated himself in the chair before the man's desk and slowly withdrew an envelope from his jacket pocket. He put it on the desk and nodded. "That's from Eleanor Whitcomb."

Humphrey's eyes flared as he leaned forward, reaching for the envelope. "Eleanor?" He dropped into his seat, grabbed the letter opener and zipped the envelope open and quickly, but nervously, withdrew the two pages of paper and began to read. He frowned, scowled at Eli, and continued reading. He looked up at Eli. "Do you know what's in this?"

"She told me. Asked me to deliver it to you. That's about all she said."

"But she's alright? Safe, I mean, unharmed?"

"She was fine when they left. She and Nathan and the baby were all fine. She said she would stay with the baby until…" He shrugged.

The banker held the letter up. "This says to send her luggage to the settlement of Alma. That's the closest to this farm of…" He looked back at the letter to see the name. "Nathan Billings? Why didn't you try to talk her out of this nonsense? She was to come here so we could be married? What kind of a man is this farmer, anyway?" he demanded.

"He seemed to be a good man, of course the grief of losing his wife and almost losing his baby showed itself, but I believe he is a good man. And as for trying to talk her out of doing what she chose, well, I kind of admire the woman for being willing to help out with a baby that definitely needed some love. Besides, it's really none of my business. She's old enough to make up her own mind about things, and we barely knew each other. It was just a happenstance that we met on the train. Now, if that's all, I'll be leaving," stated Eli, standing and extending his hand to the man to shake.

"You can't leave! What am I to do?" pleaded the man. He was used to giving orders and bending others to his will, now he had no control nor influence, and he was exasperated, waving the letter around, looking from Eli to the letter and to the window.

"Maybe you should do as she asks. If you have any other thoughts, you might take a ride to Alma and find her, or…" He shrugged and grinned, thinking *She made the right choice taking that farmer over this arrogant lump o' lard! He didn't say a word about loving her or being concerned about her as a woman. Sounded more like a busted business deal and he's a tad angry and disappointed he didn't get his way.* He shook his head as he turned to leave.

Eli opened the door and without a look back, exited the bank, a broad smile painting his face. He saw the depot when he rode into town and stopped to check on the schedule. He slipped the big watch from his pocket, checked the time, and with a few hours to spare, he led his horses across the street, slapped the leads over the hitch rail and stepped up on the boardwalk to enter the Bartell House and dining room. He made short work of beef, potatoes, and biscuits, and asked the cook to prepare some food for his train ride to Fort Hays. When the bundle of food was placed at his table, he paid the waiter and left.

The train stopped at Junction City just after midday and Eli loaded his horses and gear in the stock car that was all but empty, save one other horse. He found a seat in the second of the passenger cars and stacked his weapons and parfleche in the corner, taking the aisle seat for himself.

It was dusk when he awoke to the screeching of the brakes on the wheels of the big locomotive. He sat up, looked out the window to see the faint lights of the depot and heard the conductor call out, "Hays City, Fort Hays, we'll be stoppin' here till mornin'! Hays City," he continued his chant as he moved down the aisle of the passenger car. Eli stood and started gathering his gear to exit the car.

He stacked the gear on the corner of the platform, went to the stock car and helped the brakeman lower the ramp. Eli saddled the horses and led them from the stock car, loaded the rest of his gear and swung aboard the claybank stallion and started for Fort Hays. It was less than a couple months ago when he, his sons, and the rest of the crew had driven the herd of horses from California and delivered them to Fort Hays, but they had not spent any time here, anxious to get to the home place in Kentucky and his sons' waiting fiancées. But Eli had resisted the advances of Geneviève Devereaux, the mother of the girls who seemed to have set her sights on Eli and he wasted little time leaving the entire romantic entourage behind.

Ever since finding his boys, after the year-long search and starting the long drive from California, Eli had spent a lot of his solitary time considering what he was going to do with the rest of his life. Since his graduation from West Point, his life had been the Army, serving at posts in the west, mostly at Fort Laramie, and the entire time of war in the cavalry, the only thing he knew was the Army. But when he mustered out to be with his dying wife, then taking on the task of finding his deserter sons, this was the first time he faced a future that was not dictated by the military. When the resurgence of the Indian Wars prompted General Sheridan to offer him a job as scout for the cavalry, he gave it little thought, until he realized the farm life and raising horses was not what he was suited for, so he considered the offer a lifeline of sorts that gave him direction for his life, but he certainly did not consider it to be his purpose for the remainder of his years, yet he also knew the dangers it involved, and it might end up being his end of life career.

The most prominent feature and recognizable landmark for the fort was the stone blockhouse, the two-story structure that was the only suitable defendable building on the grounds. The dim light of dusk showed the other buildings, barracks, sutler's, offices, the few officer's quarters, the stables with the adjoining corrals and pasture, and the warehouses for supplies for this fort and others. The post's offices showed lights and some activity, so Eli pointed his horses that direction, pulled up in front and stepped down. As he was tethering his animals, a soldier, two stripes on his sleeve, came from the office, stood before the door and asked, "What's your business?"

Eli looked at the man, frowned, and glanced at the door that stood open a crack, and answered, "Wanna see Sheridan."

"That's General Sheridan, an' he ain't seein' nobody at this time o' day!"

"Corporal, I suggest you tell General Sheridan that Colonel Elijah McCain is here to see him as requested!" growled Eli, tired and a little impatient with the impertinent corporal.

The man's face dropped and his eyes flared. "Uh, sorry, Colonel, I din't know! Yessir, I'll tell the general right away, sir!" and snapped a quick salute as he turned on his heel and pushed through the door.

Eli grinned, shaking his head, as he leaned against the hitchrail, arms folded across his chest. He heard a less-than-pleasant exchange from within but could not make out the words, but the tone was sufficient to know that Phil Sheridan was not pleased with the corporal. The door quickly opened, and Eli heard the general holler, "An' get Forsyth in here, NOW!"

The corporal snapped another salute and said, "The general will see you now, sir!" and trotted off to the parade ground and the officer's quarters beyond. Eli watched the man go and stepped into the open doorway, "Eli! Glad you made it, an' just in time! Be seated!" stated the general, a broad grin splitting his face.

CHAPTER 8

ORDERS

General Sheridan dropped his eyes to the papers on his desk, drew a deep breath that lifted his shoulders and lifted his eyes to look from Brevet Colonel Forsyth to Eli and began, "Forsyth, I know you know what I'm about to say, but this is for Eli's information." He paused and looked gravely at Eli. "We started getting reports from the acting governor of Colorado territory, Frank Hall, that the Cheyenne and Arapaho are running amok throughout the plains 'tween here an' there. Last report showed a tally of seventy-nine settlers had been killed on repeated attacks on farms an' such. Ain't nobody safe from attack." He grumbled a little, looked at the two men and continued, "Now, we been keepin' busy with other attacks, and I've been focusing on the country south of the Arkansas. The Seventh has been handlin' that, and I've got the Tenth 'tween the Republican and Smoky Hill Rivers. Now, Colonel Forsyth did as I ordered an' recruited a bunch o' ornery scouts from Fort Harker and here at Hays, 'bout forty-eight of 'em, all good men. He has Lieutenant

Beecher as his exec and Eli. I want you to go with him. He'll be in command, and you'll be, well, kind of an adviser, what with your Indian experience, and if necessary, and anything happens to him, you'll be his second in command. Since you're scoutin', you won't be in uniform an' that's what you said you preferred, right?" he asked, and Eli responded with a nod.

"There's no tellin' what you might run into. We've heard there's Lakota, Cheyenne, Arapaho, and even some Kiowa. An' most o' them Cheyenne are Dog Soldiers and both o' you know about them. You leave with first light. Any questions?" he asked, glancing from one to the other of the men.

The general stood, prompting the two men before him to do the same. He extended his hand to shake with each man and wished them, "Good hunting! Oh, and..." addressing himself to Eli alone, "at your insistence, I signed on Charlie Two Toes. He'll be the only native scout among the bunch."

"That's good, General. He's a good man and will be a credit to the outfit."

Forsyth stood staring, growled, "You signed on an Indian?"

"He's a Pawnee. I rode with him all the way from California, and he has good experience and will be an asset."

Forsyth grumbled and turned away, but his disdain for the native was immediately evident and told Eli a lot about the man. When he exited the office, Sheridan motioned for Eli to stay a moment and motioned him to the chair as he also seated himself. He began, "Eli, we've fought together and know each other pretty well. Now I've also fought with Forsyth and he's a good officer, but he's lacking in experience with the Indians, and he's known to be a bit set in his ways, stubborn, you know the type. That's why I want you with them, just in case he gets into more trouble than he can handle." He paused, looked to Eli from under his bushy brows, and added, "But don't you say a word to him about our conversation, understand?"

"I do, sir." The two men stood, shook hands, and with a nod and a wave, bid their goodbyes.

————

WITH THE RISING sun at their back, the shadows of the company of scouts stretched out before them as they rode from Fort Hays. Forsyth had dispatched two scouts, George Culver and Bill Wilson, to lead the way. Their basic route would be to move southwest to the Smoky Hill River and follow it west to Fort Wallace. This would be a time when the men would get acquainted with one another, and as was the way with fighting men, find out who they thought they could trust to side them in a fight and who might not stand his ground. Every man was armed with the Spencer repeaters, and some carried additional weapons, as did Eli, never without his Colt revolving shotgun nor his Winchester Yellow Boy rifle. Eli rode his claybank stallion, but was without the grey packhorse, leaving him at the stables at Fort Hays, all the men carried their own rations, but there were also ample provisions carried on the four pack mules.

Eli rode beside Forsyth and the younger man often cast glances his way. Eli knew the planned route was to go southwest, follow the Smoky Hill River, but they were going northwest. He frowned as he glanced to Forsyth, wondering what he was planning. Eli was curious of the Brevet Colonel, although his regular rank was major, but he chose to let the commander take the lead in orders and conversation. They rode silently for the first half day until Forsyth looked sidelong at Eli and asked, "So you're a West Point man?"

"That's right, class of '48," answered Eli. "You?"

"Came up through the ranks, enlisted in '61, Chicago Volunteer Dragoons. Mustered out after three months, received a commission to First Lieutenant in eighth Illinois Cavalry, fought with the Army of the Potomac, was aide-de-camp with Sheridan in Shenandoah Valley. Made Brevet Brigadier at the end of the war, then after that, major in Ninth Cavalry."

"Impressive." A glance toward the man told Eli that he was quite proud of his accomplishments, as he should be, but there was something more about the man. His personality and manner of command showed him to be a man of force, unbending in his attitude and unwilling to listen to others of lesser rank and often showed some disdain for others of equal or higher rank. It was not uncommon for those that rose through the ranks to attain their position to resent those that came from West Point or received commissions through political influence. Eli had served with officers from both camps and soon realized it was not the background or social position nor wealth that made a man a good officer, but something deeper called character and respect for his fellow man, qualities that he did not immediately see in Forsyth.

But Forsyth did show himself to be a capable officer, always vigilant, ensuring there were competent scouts out before the column, ample guards posted at night, and appropriate care was given for the men regarding supplies and more. Yet they had traveled for two days, always bearing basically northwest and not always in a direct route, often taking to the swales and lowlands, not showing themselves in the rolling hills of the flats. But as the scouts would return after a half day, Forsyth would quiz them, sometimes showing disappointment at their failure to find fresh sign of any hostiles.

After the scouts returned at the end of the third day, Eli listened to the quizzing of Forsyth, saw his consternation, and knew he was not just leading the men to Fort Wallace as ordered, he was looking for a fight. He wanted to find some hostiles and show them what his troop of scouts were capable of doing, or maybe it was just to add a tally of kills and glory to his own record. Eli recognized this hunger for glory having seen it in the eyes and manner of many officers and others in the war and wherever it showed itself, death followed and all too often it was not just the death of the enemy. Yet he also knew, when a leader showed disdain for the enemy, it warped his judgment prompting him to take unnecessary risks. He had seen it many times before, especially when it came to Indian fighting. Many officers had been so indoctrinated about the lesser natives and their inability to mount a proper tactical assault or defense that those same officers assumed the native leaders to be incompetent, and that prejudicial presumption often resulted in unnecessary losses.

Some of the country was looking familiar to Eli, remembering just a couple months past when he and his crew drove the herd of remounts from California to Fort Hays. He most often led the herd or scouted well ahead and made himself familiar with the country, and he recognized some of the landmarks. He remembered Sheridan telling them to follow the Smoky Hill River, which was well south of where they were, although they had talked about the raids of the Cheyenne on the Saline,

Solomon and Republican rivers and they were now crossing what he recognized as Prairie Dog Creek and this morning's crossing had been of the Solomon. He shook his head, thinking that Forsyth was going well out of his way to find a fight with the natives, all the while thinking that the aide-de-camp of General Sheridan had seen very little of the bloody battles in the war, usually staying behind the lines with the general in his camp. And none of those fights would begin to resemble the fights with the Cheyenne or Arapaho. What he had not seen was the bloody remains of a native attack that left behind mutilated bodies, burned corpses, and worse. Eli was certain if he had ever witnessed that kind of battle and the remains afterward, he might not be so quick to pick a fight with these warriors of the plains.

It was late on the fourth day when Forsyth finally ordered the men into camp. When Eli and Lieutenant Beecher joined Forsyth at his fire, the Brevet Colonel began. "We have not found any fresh sign of raiding parties. I believe they got word of our being in the vicinity, and they went to ground. Could expect nothing less from the cowardly redskins," he grumbled, tossing a stick into the fire. "On the morrow, we will turn south and make for Fort Wallace. That will put us in on the evening of the 5th of September. Hopefully, we'll get a day or two of rest, but if word comes of any attacks, we'll be the first to take the field." He paused, looked around the fire at the two officers, First Sergeant Bill McCall, and acting assistant surgeon J.H. Mooers, then offered cups of hot coffee to each and poured them all himself.

Eli asked, "How far do you reckon it to be to Wallace?"

"Jack Donovan was our lead scout today and he's quite familiar with this area. He says it's a good day's ride, about forty miles, but with an early start we'll make it shortly after nightfall," declared the colonel, letting a slight smirk turn up the corner of his mouth. He knew full well that he had been pushing the men hard since they left Fort Hays, as twenty miles was considered a good day's ride, but he added, "Yes, I've been pushing the men. If we strike a trail of hostiles, we'll have to move fast to apprehend them."

"You know, of course, that tired men and tired horses can be a detriment to a fighting force," offered Eli.

The colonel sneered at him and answered, "You let me worry about that, McCain."

CHAPTER 9

PURSUIT

I t was a tired group of men that dragged into the grounds of Fort Wallace. But tired or not, the men were wise enough to tend to their animals, stripping the gear, rubbing them down and getting them grain and water, before rolling out their bedrolls and turning in for the night. Any conversation was little more than grunts and groans, as Eli looked at his pocket watch to see it was nearing midnight when he finally stretched out and pulled the blanket over his tired body. Charlie Two Toes was already stretched out, laying with his hands behind his head and looking at the stars. As Eli lay back, Charlie glanced around and seeing no one near, quietly asked Eli, "So, what'chu think 'bout the colonel?"

"Humph," grunted Eli, trying to make himself comfortable.

"Yup," responded Charlie, and turned to his side to get some sleep.

FOR SEVERAL DAYS, the men spent the time tending to their horses, doctoring any sores, replacing shoes, basically spoiling the animals with attention. When not in the stables or corrals, the men worked on their gear, cleaned their weapons, restocked their Blakeslee loaders with ammunition, and ferreted away any extra garnered provisions. By the end of the fourth day, the men were getting restless, but none were anxious to resume the forced rides of forty miles a day. Early on the morning of September 10th, a rider came into the fort asking for the commander. Although the fort's commander was Captain H. C. Bankhead, when the rider asked for the commander, Brevet Colonel Forsyth stepped forward. "I'm Colonel Forsyth. What's the problem?"

"I'm with a freighting outfit back at end-of-track for the Kansas-Pacific railroad. We were attacked by a war party of Injuns—had two men kilt, bunch o' our mules were run off. We was promised protection an' we cain't build no railroad with them Injuns about!" growled the messenger. "So, wha'chu gonna do, Colonel?" he taunted.

"We're going after 'em, of course!" answered a grinning Forsyth. He turned to Lieutenant Beecher. "Ready the men! Every man is to have two full Blakeslees, rations for six days, and pack the mules with extra rations, ammunition, medical supplies and whatever else we might need! We leave in one hour!" The grinning Forsyth looked at the messenger. "How far to end-of-track?"

"Half-day's ride," answered the surprised messenger. "But I ain't goin'! I'm gettin' sumpin' to eat and get some rest. I been ridin' half the night." He turned, grabbed the lead of his horse, and stomped away.

FORSYTH SAT erect in his saddle as he faced the men of the band now known as Forsyth Scouts. He looked down the ranks of the less that military disciplined band of frontiersmen and began, "Men, now you'll get a chance to earn that $50 you'll be getting. A raiding party of Indians hit end-of-track of the railroad about a half-day's ride from here—killed two men and ran off some stock. They said it was a good-sized party estimated to be about twenty-five strong. We will track them down and wipe them out!" his voice rose almost to a shout as he emphasized wiping them out. His nostrils flared and he came off the seat of his saddle, standing in his stirrups, looking up and down the ranks of the men.

"You are supposed to be Indian fighters! You will get your chance to prove it!" He jerked the head of his mount around, dug spurs into the horse's ribs and with a wave and a shout, "Let's go!" and the group of men, many older than Forsyth, followed, most shaking their heads and looking at one another, chuckling at the antics of their leader.

The trail of the marauders was plainly visible and with a quick stop at end-of-track to talk to the rail crew, Forsyth started the band of scouts after the war party. Even with the sun lowering in the west, the tall grass was trampled under the hurried passage of the raiders and was easily followed. With the South Fork of the Smoky Hill River off their left shoulder, they soon crossed Sand Creek and continued northwest close on the trail. But dusk soon dropped its curtain and Forsyth reluctantly called for stopping and making camp for the night.

Lieutenant called out, "Burke, Ranahan, you're

standing first guard, Stubbs, Oaks, you're second up, Hurst and Lyden, you're last guard!"

Each of the men answered with a "Yo!" and made ready for their watch.

Each guard would be for two hours before relieving the next watch. The horses were kept near each man, although stripped, rubbed down, and picketed. Yet the six hours passed quickly, and the eastern sky showed a thin line of grey when the men were rolled out for the morning. Their only breakfast was whatever they had left over from the night before and the colonel had them all in the saddle before the last stars snuffed out their lanterns.

With the lieutenant serving as Executive Officer to Colonel Forsyth, Eli had dropped back and rode beside Charlie Two Toes. The early hours of the morning were chilly, and the men hunkered in their coats, their horses walking with heads lowered, breath showing in the morning cold, but the group rode silent, horses' hooves shuffling in the grass, saddles creaking, and only an occasional blow from a horse or groan from a man. This was a time when men's thoughts chase possibilities, prompting the men to search the distant flats. Although it appeared that there was nothing but a long flat line of horizon that showed as a shadow in the distance, these seasoned men knew the slight roll of the land could hide a hundred warriors who would rise from the grass in an instant. Occasionally a hand would drop to the butt of a scabbarded rifle and the man would stand in his stirrups, but with a look of relief, would drop back into the seat of his saddle and look around to see if anyone had witnessed his moment of fear.

By noon of the second day, the trail began to fade, not from lack of use, but because the raiders had split up, leaving the trail in different directions and small numbers, oftentimes no more than one or two splitting off and fading into the distance. When the scouts, George Oakes and Tom Murphy, returned, they stated the obvious. "Colonel, those Injuns done went ever which-away. Ain't no trail that has more'n two or three. But…" He paused, took a deep breath. "Me'n Oakes both think they're headin' the same way, which is northwest, just like we been goin'."

Oakes added, "We seen that before, Colonel. That's what they usually do, cuz they either know we're followin' 'em, or they just assume that somebody is followin'. They most often split up and scatter, comin' back together at some pre-determined place."

Eli came forward and now sat, hands on the pommel of his saddle as he waited for Forsyth to speak, but was surprised when the colonel looked his way and asked, "That the way you have it figured, McCain?"

Eli just nodded, refusing to acknowledge the colonel's lack of military decorum by referring to him in front of the men by using only his last name. He clinched his teeth, his jaw muscles flexing, knowing he out-ranked the major whose current rank was Brevet Colonel, which was temporary, but Eli chose not to make it an issue, choosing to remain as a scout with no visible rank, but he also knew all the men knew Eli was the ranking officer.

Colonel Forsyth nodded, looking at the scouts. "We'll keep going. Return to your scouting and keep a close watch in the distance. I think they'll come back together and if they know we're following, it'll probably to make an ambush, so watch yourselves."

The two scouts nodded, wheeled their horses around

and took off at a lope to make their scout well ahead of the body of men.

The next day, the colonel doubled the scout sending out Barney Day, Eli Ziegler, John Lyden, and Jack Stillwell. "I want you men to fan out, keep your eyes open in the distance, but watch close at hand for any fresh sign of hostiles. We'll be comin' up to the Republican River today, and I'm thinking they might be somewhere close to water and that would be a likely place. As soon as any of you see sign, you skedaddle back here and let us know! Got that?"

"We do, sir," answered Stillwell, speaking for the four scouts. He had become one of the more respected men and had proven himself to be a better than most tracker.

The colonel pushed the men harder on this, the fourth day, as they neared the Republican River and stopped for their nooning. They had moved without stopping, save for a short stretch when the colonel had the men walking with their horses to give the animals a bit of a break, and Eli guessed they had covered at least twenty miles when some of the men approached him and asked, "Eli, that Forsyth has been pushin' mighty hard. If we come on them Injuns now, we'll be so dadgummed tired we'd probably give up just so's we could get some rest! Can you do anything about it?"

Eli shook his head, looking at the men, and answered, "Men, he's the man in charge and as you know, all of us have to do what he says. I suggest you do your best to be wary, don't let your tiredness make you lazy and careless, that won't do any of us any good. I'll see if I can drop a suggestion here and there, but if we cut sign, there's no tellin' what'll happen."

"But it not just the pushin', we're gettin' all fired low on supplies. We been out four days now an' we only brought six days of rations, an' hungry men don't fight all that well," mumbled Henry Tucker, the self-appointed spokesman for the group.

The men had no sooner finished their nooning than the colonel had them back in the saddle. Shortly after the group started out, one of the scouts, Jack Stillwell, came riding back at a lope, slid to a stop beside the colonel and his report was heard by most as they all came closer. "Colonel, we done found fresh sign, like you figgered, by the Republican and it looks to be more'n we been followin'."

Forsyth let a broad grin split his face as he grimaced and slapped the pommel of his saddle. "I knew it!" He gathered himself and looked at the scout with a stoic expression. "How far?"

"Couple hours," answered Stillwell, reining his mount around to side the colonel, who kept moving.

"Good, good!" He turned in his saddle and gave the arm pumping signal for quick time and kicked his mount up to a trot.

The men, with a little more than the usual grumbling, followed their leader and talked among themselves. The land was flat, bunch grass, cacti, yucca, sage, and low rolling hills that offered little if any cover. The blue canopy held few clouds and the sun bore down from the brassy sky giving no quarter to the tired horses. After about a mile they dropped back to a steady walk, but after the report all the men were considerably more vigilant. The second guard, Barney Day, sat his mount, waiting for the column to come close and stepped down, motioning to the sign near the trail. The colonel reined up, stepped down and Barney motioned to the tracks.

"Look there, Colonel, those are drag marks for travois. There's plenty of 'em too. That says they're travelin' with their women and there's a lot more of 'em than we were followin' from that attack."

Eli and Charlie had also stepped down, walked up to see the tracks and as Barney was reporting to the colonel, Eli and Charlie were down on one knee, examining the tracks as well. The two talked quietly between them and Eli stood and walked to the colonel.

"Colonel, lookin' at those tracks, they're not only travelin' with their families and draggin' their lodges, this is the whole village and maybe more. I'd guess there are at least a hundred, maybe more."

While they spoke, several of the others had moved closer to the sign and looked at the trail made by the villagers. They talked among themselves and were visibly concerned.

The colonel looked at Eli. "That's what we've been hunting! Catching up to a small war party would do little to stop these continual attacks, but if we can wipe out a whole village, maybe then they'll understand the futility of fighting against us! That's what General Sherman wanted to do, eliminate all resistance and get them all on the reservations. That's the only thing they'll respond to, when enough of them are destroyed, they'll give up!" The more he spoke, the more his words and expression showed his vehemence and hatred. Eli shook his head, recalling other times when leaders led their men to wholesale slaughter, fighting with an unreasonable blood lust, and this was something he would not be a part of nor tolerate.

CHAPTER 10

SCOUT

Another early start on the fifth day of trailing the marauders saw the men with the slow rising sun off their right shoulders with a promise of a hot day, but the cool air of morning afforded some relief. They crossed the South Fork of the Republican River and the trail of the natives continued to the northwest, and Forsyth and Beecher rode side by side, often talking animatedly and motioning to the tracks.

Eli turned to Charlie. "Those two are about as excited as a pair of magpies looking at a fresh carcass!"

"And that ain't good for the rest of us," answered Charlie. He had been talking to some of the other scouts and most were in agreement that they were headed for trouble. "Look there," stated Charlie, pointing at another trail of several riders, also with travois, which joined the track they were following.

"Ummhmm, I saw it, and this trail is talkin' to me." He looked sidelong at Charlie. "How 'bout you'n me tellin' the colonel we'll take the scout after noonin'?"

"I was thinkin' the same thing. I'm not too confident

in some o' these scouts. I been watchin' and some of 'em that say they're scouts, prob'ly couldn't find their way out of an outhouse!" grumbled Charlie.

Eli chuckled. "Well, most of 'ems alright, but I've noticed some can track, but can't read what's bein' said by the trail. Know what I mean?"

"Yup," mumbled Charlie. "An' that could get us all in a peck o' trouble."

They crossed a dry creek bed that lay between the bluffs of the rolling hills. After topping out on the north side, the dry land seemed to stretch into the hazy distance farther than eye could see, but a pair of dust devils danced across the flat, unhindered by trees or hills, scattering tumbleweeds across the plains. The men tucked their chins in their neckerchiefs, lifted the collars of their jackets and peered through squinted eyes at the colonel and his exec as they faded in and out of view in the dust clouds.

Eli guessed they had traveled close to twenty miles when the signal was given to stop for their nooning. There was an almost dry riverbed that Charlie recognized. "That's the Arikaree. We crossed that comin' out, remember?"

"Doesn't it run into the Republican a little farther north?" asked Eli.

"That's the one," answered Charlie as they reined up at a cluster of twisted cottonwoods that showed their rough grey trunks, dead branches, and skimpy greenery.

The men scrounged through their saddlebags to get the makings for their noon meal, and with a handful of jerky, Eli walked to where the colonel and Beecher sat under the shade of a stunted hackberry.

As he neared, Eli began, "Colonel, how 'bout me'n Charlie taking the scout after we eat, give the others a bit of a break. Charlie knows this country pretty good and might be a help."

"Nothin' special to know is there? This is the North Fork of the Republican, and from the looks of things, the sign shows the natives movin' upstream."

Eli slowly nodded, choosing not to correct the colonel on his assumptions. "Well, this country has its own way of changin' and foolin' riders. We came over this way with our trail drive just a few weeks back and Charlie's people hunted this country. It wouldn't hurt to get another look at things."

"Alright but keep us posted on anything you see. The other scouts just came in and said the tracks on the other side"—nodding to the nearby riverbed—"show more natives joinin' the others."

The returning scouts, Fletcher Vilott and Sigman Schlesinger, after reporting to the colonel and learning they would be staying with the group, went to the other men and told what they had seen. "I'm telling you, there are more Injuns comin' from the north that's joinin' the others, can't tell how many there are now, but that trail is wide'rn a couple wagons end to end, and the grass is trampled down into the dirt!"

The other men mumbled among themselves, with tidbits of remarks heard that told the men were more than just concerned. "That could mean hunnerds o' them red devils!" grumbled one, another added, "However many, there's a durn sight more of 'em than there are of us!"

"I think we need to skedaddle outta here, that's what I'm thinkin'!"

"What say we just go to the colonel an' let him know what we think!" declared John Hurst, one of the more outspoken of the men. His suggestion met with nodding heads and comments of agreement and the group seemed to move as one as they started to the hackberry tree where the colonel and his exec were taking their meal. As they neared, the colonel saw them coming and stood with a scowl on his face, demanding, "What's this all about?"

Hurst stepped forward. "Colonel, we don't think you're considerin' ever'thing." He motioned across the riverbed. "Those tracks are showin' there's a whole big bunch o' them Injuns in that pack and we're outnumbered by maybe five or six to one! And we're 'bout outta rations an' we ain't too happy 'bout takin' on that many! Now, we ain't affeered of a fight, but that's more'n what we bargained for!" His remarks elicited nodding heads and grumbles of agreement.

The colonel stood quiet for a moment, looking at the men, glancing from one to the other, then stated, "Did you not enlist to fight Indians?"

"Well, yeah, but..."

"No buts about it. You signed up to fight Indians and we're gonna fight Indians." Without saying as much, all knew he implied that if they did not fight, they would be branded as cowards. He paused, looking at the chastised and slightly humbled men. "None of us know for sure how many warriors are in this bunch we're following, and McCain and Charlie Two Toes are going to be scouting this afternoon and maybe they'll be able to give us a more accurate report than just 'the trail's gettin' bigger.' Now, you men get your noonin' done and we'll get back on the trail. We'll be going upstream of this river and maybe find a better camp for tonight." Several of the men grumbled, but all turned back to their horses and gear and prepared to take to the trail again.

Eli and Charlie crossed the riverbed and turned

upstream to the southwest. The trail of the natives had grown larger but kept to the lowland below the bluffs that rose on the northwest side of the river. In places, there were deeper pools in the riverbed, the little stream continued its trickling flow that was more of a creek than a river, and the sign showed the natives often stopping for water or to water their animals as they moved. Charlie pointed to a muddy bank that showed many tracks. "That tells me they are in no hurry!"

Eli reined up, sat with arms folded across his pommel as he looked at the tracks, and lanced to Charlie. "Now, back there a couple days, the raiders split up and scattered like they knew or thought they were being followed. But now, it's as if they want us to follow, no effort to cover their trail, nothing showin' they're in a hurry, makes me think they're baitin' a trap."

"I was thinkin' the same thing," replied Charlie, looking to the bluffs that rose off their right shoulder.

These were not high bluffs, rising only about a hundred feet higher than the river bottom, but if there were any basins, valleys of the like beyond this long line of bluffs, the entire band of several hundred would be out of sight of anyone that followed the river.

Charlie looked to Eli. "You thinkin' what I'm thinkin'?"

"You think we can get up there without bein' seen?"

"There's a cut yonder that we can try," pointing to the break in the bluffs on the right.

"After you!" declared Eli, surrendering the lead to Charlie.

They moved slowly up the long draw, ever vigilant for they were in the bottom of the cut and little protection or cover was offered. As they neared the upper end, Charlie held up his hand, reined up and stepped down.

He walked back to Eli, spoke softly, "I'm gonna crawl up there, have a look-see."

"Wait, let me give you my binoculars," answered Eli, reaching back to his saddlebags.

Eli took the reins of Charlie's horse and watched as the Pawnee dropped to a crouch and quickly moved near the top of the ridge, bellied down, and crawled to the top. Charlie lifted the binoculars and began to scan the rolling flats. He twisted about, looking to scan the entire flats, slowly searching the distant basins. He lay still for a few moments, crabbed back below the ridge and rose to return to Eli.

"We'll need to go further upstream, then try again. These bluffs give way to a long valley, broad basin, that creek we just passed that came from that way meanders for a spell and looks like there might be a likely place for a big encampment."

"Then let's get a move on 'fore the colonel catches up and gets us in trouble."

The sun was lowering in the west and painted the sky in shades of orange when Eli and Charlie crawled up another bluff to search the flats. Eli had the binoculars in hand, but what lay before them could easily be seen without the aid of the field glasses. The wide basin held over two hundred lodges, probably more, a horse herd grazed on the far edge of the basin and appeared to be almost as big as the herd Eli and Charlie had driven from California. There were cookfires flaring, but the women had wisely chosen dead and dry wood that gave little or no smoke. As they watched, a band of riders numbering about a dozen, came into the village from the direction of the Arikaree but farther upstream than where Eli and Charlie had left the river. Eli looked at Charlie and both nodded as they began crabbing back off the edge of the bluff to return to their horses.

When they started from the draw, both men were silent, thinking about the massive village that held both Cheyenne, Arapaho, and maybe some Lakota. They were considering what was before them and when they came to the mouth of the draw, they turned back downstream, kicked their mounts to a lope and headed for the band of scouts. The band had camped no more than a couple miles downstream from where Eli and Charlie had mounted the bluffs, and as they came into the camp, they spotted Forsyth and Beecher and rode directly to them. Both men stepped down and Eli looked around, wanting his report to the colonel to be just between them, and began. "Colonel, just beyond that ridge"—nodding to the bluff behind the camp of the scouts—"there are anywhere from three to five hundred, maybe more, Cheyenne, Arapaho and maybe some Lakota, warriors. And they know we're here. While we watched, a bunch of their warriors came from upstream here"—pointing to the southwest of the valley—"and gave their report. I think they've been waiting on us to catch up and were layin' in wait upstream."

Eli waited for some response from the colonel, but all he saw was a slow grin painting the face of the man who had been wanting to get into a fight with the natives.

Eli slowly shook his head and started to turn away when Forsyth said, "Good report. Thanks, McCain. We should be able to catch up to 'em and hit 'em hard!"

Eli dropped his eyes, shook his head, and turned away.

CHAPTER 11

SANDBAR

The colonel had put the word out that every man was to picket his horse and ensure the pickets were deep and tight, and to "keep your saddle and gear close to hand, we might hafta move in a hurry!" The word had also spread about the report given by Eli and Charlie about the number of natives in the nearby encampment and all the men were restless, fearing what might come with the dawning. Their camp was in the shadow of the bluff just north of the river where the shallow Arikaree split to form the island in the middle of the riverbed. There was ample grass for all the horses, scattered trees for shelter but very little real cover in the event of a fight.

Eli and Charlie had picketed their horses at the edge of the bluff on the downstream end of the camp, closer to the confluence of the Black Wolf Creek and the Arikaree. When they shook out their bedrolls beside a scrubby piñon, Eli stepped closer to Charlie. "I been thinkin' Charlie, and I don't like what I'm comin' up with."

Charlie chuckled. "I think we been thinkin' the same thing, Eli."

"When we saw that band returning to the camp and the gestures they were making, I think they were the advance scout for an attack, and they were none too happy that we didn't keep goin'. But they won't give up on the idea. Now, there's a bit of a shoulder on that bluff yonder, 'bout halfway up the camp. Now, neither one of us are on Forsyth's enlistment rolls, since we were recruited and signed by Sheridan separately, and if you go missing, they won't think anything. So, if that attack comes and is as big as I think, I'm gonna shiny up that knob yonder and do my shootin' from up there. Meanwhile, I think you need to skedaddle back to Fort Wallace or thereabouts and try to find some help. Forsyth is too stubborn to do that right away, he thinks he can whip the whole Cheyenne Nation by himself, and I think we might need some help gettin' that done!"

"You want mc to leave now?" asked Charlie, showing a little eagerness.

Eli chuckled. "No, only if we are attacked, then git!"

They stretched out on their bedrolls, both laying with hands clasped behind their heads and watching as the stars lit their lanterns for the night. Charlie pointed to the Milky Way. "My people believe that is the trail to the everlasting. When a good warrior dies, he travels that trail to the land of our ancestors."

"Well, I believe that God placed all the stars in the heavens as He said in the first book of the Bible where He said, *Let there be lights in the firmament of the Heaven to divide the day from the night and let them be for signs, and for seasons, and for days, and years: And let them be for lights in the firmament of the Heaven to give light upon the earth: and it was so*. And when He was done He said, *it was good.* "

"I can certainly agree with that!" answered Charlie and waved his hand across the night sky and said, "It is good!" and chuckled.

It was a restless night for all the men, the sentries were especially restless, and it was still dark when Eli rolled from his blankets, saddled his horse and strapped down his gear, took the Spencer and his Bible and started for the shoulder of rock that he had chosen for his promontory. He thought to himself as he left Rusty ground tied, *I'll spend a little time with the Lord and when daylight comes, I'll come back for Rusty and then..."* He shrugged and started up the slight slope, aiming for the escarpment of rock that showed shadows in the moonlight.

He pushed his way through the grass and yucca, stepped up on the rocks, and climbed to the top of the shoulder. He seated himself beside the twisted cedar, made himself comfortable and lifted his eyes to the heavens and began to pray, but he had barely said a few quiet words, when the moonlight showed movement in the tall grass at the upper end of the camp, near the bend of the river. He leaned forward, shaded his eyes in the darkness, and watched. One, no, two, no, more, figures were crawling in the grass toward the camp. Eli lifted his Spencer, used the twisted branch of the cedar for a rest and took aim. Even with the dim light, the brass button of the front sight settled on the lead figure and Eli took a breath, let out a little, and began to squeeze the trigger. The Spencer barked and bucked, the blast reverberating along the bluff, and was quickly echoed by other rifles firing from the cover of rocks, trees and humps. Fire stabbed the darkness, screams of war cries rippled through the grass, and shouts of warning, "Indians! Indians!" came from the men in the camp.

Pandemonium prevailed as figures rose from the grass to charge the cluster of men and horses at the base of the bluff. Spencer rifles barked and blasted, and the thunder of hooves vibrated the very ground they sat upon as a band of mounted and screaming warriors came charging from the darkness to be met by the unyielding wall of lead from the continually repeating .52 caliber Spencer rifles fired by the frightened but determined band of scouts.

The sun was at the back of the scouts, casting their position in shadows and darkness, making it hard for the charging Cheyenne, Arapaho, and Lakota warriors to find a single target. They fired their rifles, some muzzle-loaders that belched lead and clouds of smoke, some repeaters like the scouts own Spencers, although those were few, and others were screaming and firing arrows and sending feathered lances flying through the air. The warriors were bedecked in their most intimidating attire, full feathered war bonnets with long trailing feathers, bone hair-pipe chest plates, buffalo rawhide war shields, war paint on both the warriors and the horses, and they charged on wide-eyed horses with flaring nostrils and open mouths and flying hooves, their war cries screamed in a cacophony of shrills and shrieks that were meant to strike fear in the hearts of their enemies and it was succeeding.

But the men of Forsyth's Scouts refused to yield their ground nor give way to any charge, meeting each assault with a barrage of rapid fire from the Spencers. Each man had two Blakeslee boxes of reloading tubes, each holding seven rounds. When their hammer clicked on an empty chamber, they quickly lowered the rifle, popped open the butt and shoved a tube with seven more rounds, slammed the butt plate, jacked a round, cocked the hammer and let the lead fly.

At the beginning of the assault, Eli saw four or five natives going after the horses of the men, he brought the Spencer to bear on one, saw him drop, but the others quickly shielded themselves with the horses and grabbed the picket pins, jerked on the leads and grabbed the manes of a horse on either side to hang suspended between the two making it impossible for Eli to take a shot, and the small band made off with five or six of the horses.

Forsyth saw the horses taken, shouted orders to the men. "Saddle your horses!" and the men instantly set about gearing up the horses, standing beside them to await more orders, with each man looking upstream waiting for another charge. Eli stood, shouted, "Look up the river!" and motioned upstream. Forsyth and the others looked but could not see as much as Eli who was atop the escarpment and shouted, "There's hundreds of 'em and they're readying another charge!"

Forsyth had realized their camp, although comfortable as a camp, was hard to defend with little or no cover offered. He stood tall and shouted, "To the sandbar! NOW!" and directed the band of scouts to take to the island where there were trees, thickets of willows, and more that would give immediate cover. "Tie off your mounts, keep them close!" he ordered as the men scattered and splashed across the little creek, going to the island and ducking behind the brush and trees. "Start digging firing pits and pile the diggin's for cover!" ordered Forsyth. Eli grinned as he heard the order, pleased with the discipline of the colonel.

The warriors were moving into position for their attack. It was evident to Eli what they planned, with many of the warriors on foot, dropping into the tall grass on either side of the river, they would take position on the banks of the river opposite the sandbar, while the bulk of the warriors, mounted, would make an all-out frontal assault. While the defenders were focused on the charge, the snipers from the grass would cut them down. But Eli kept his eyes on the warriors in the grass, mentally mapping those on his side of the river, and even some on the far side. Eli stayed where he was, believing he would have a better field of fire, at least for now and could offer covering fire for the men.

Within moments, the assault began, the screams of war cries brought the heads of the scouts up from their digging and grabbed rifles, readying for the charge. Forsyth barked, "Don't shoot till I do! We'll wait till they're about fifty yards out, then cut 'em down!"

He repeated the order as he faced those on the far side and further back, then dropped behind to cover himself. The thunder of the charging warriors was felt as the scouts hunkered in their gun pits, with five or six hundred mounted warriors making the charge, the ground rolled, and thunder bounced across the river bottom.

Screams of war cries split the air and the shouts of warriors hurling insults in their native tongue bounced off the hillsides. It was a rolling tide of war bonnets, feathered lances, painted faces and clattering hooves that swelled across the narrow valley and grew as the warriors neared.

Forsyth shouted, "Hold...Hold...hold..." drawing out the command as men held their breath, squinted their eyes and narrowed their aim until, "FIRE!!" and the blast of fifty Spencer .52 caliber rifles bucked, bellowed, and belched a lead wall that drove into the swelling tide, painting bare skinned warriors with their own blood as they fell under the hooves of their fellow warriors' war horses, to be trampled under and driven into the grassy soil.

Scattered firing came from the grasses and Eli began picking his targets, driving the crawling snipers into the grass, never to rise again as they painted the grass with their blood, brains, and guts. He fired, fired, fired, and fired again. Each time carefully picking his targets. Whenever he saw movement, smoke from a fired rifle, a feather that contrasted with the green of the grass, he sent a messenger of death to stop the progress of that warrior.

CHAPTER 12

BATTLE

The charge of the mounted warriors swept by the island, yet to the scouts the line of attackers seemed endless. The barrage continued and the scouts reloaded and fired their weapons with such speed and precision, the barrels of the Spencers were hot and when the water of the creek was splashed so that water hit the barrels, it sizzled into steam in an instant. The men continued to fire, taking careful aim with each trigger pull and often seeing the target do a backward somersault off their racing horse, but the warriors following neither swerved, stopped, nor slowed their charge, giving little heed to their fallen warriors.

The stench of gun smoke, death, blood, puke, mud and trampled bodies hung like a fog over the battlefield, men choking on the stench and more. When the charge began to wane, Eli watched the warriors continue on the run past the island and swerve into the cut of the hills that carried the waters of Black Wolf Creek. Even many of those in the grasses had risen and run, climbing the hills downriver of the island and disappearing.

With a thorough look around, Eli moved back from his rocky escarpment, backed away through the tall grass and cholla, caught up the reins of Rusty and leaned low on the claybank's neck as he dug heels into his ribs and encouraged the horse, "Let's go boy! We need to get to cover—quick!" The big stallion lunged off the face of the hill, splashed across the creek with one long stride, and crashed through the willows as Eli shouted, "Hold your fire! It's me—McCain!"

When they hit the cluster of trees, Eli reined up, dropped to the ground and positioned Rusty behind the trees as best he could, loosened the girth and with the shotgun slung on one shoulder and the Spencer in his hand, he started to the upstream end of the island where he had last seen Forsyth.

———

THE CHIEFS, war leaders, medicine men, and prominent warriors had gathered in a circle in the midst of the warriors who were examining their wounds, grumbling among themselves, and letting women nurse their injuries. There was an air of anger among the leaders as one of the chiefs stood before the others.

"Who started the fight?" growled the chief who stood with arms across his chest and a sneer on his face. The attack had been planned in every detail and the chiefs were to give the order for the first assault, but someone had moved early and tried to capture the horses of the white men and were seen and fired upon. That eliminated any surprise the chiefs had planned, and there was anger stewing around the circle of leaders.

The war leader of the Cheyenne. "It was White Weasel Bear! He was to lead the warriors that were to capture the horses but was seen and killed. The son of his brother, White Thunder, tried to stop him, but he too was killed."

"What are these rifles the white men use that fire so many times?" asked one of the chiefs of the Arapaho.

"I saw the same as this!" shouted another, hefting his recently stolen Spencer. "But I do not know how they reload so many and so fast! It must be different!" he declared.

"We have lost many and many more"—motioning to the numbers of wounded that were being tended by the women—"have taken bullets and might not live."

Another war leader stood, pointed with his chin to a prominent warrior opposite the circle, and asked, "Where was *xénéhe*, Roman Nose, the great warrior of the Cheyenne that so many think is the greatest warrior? Did anyone see him during the charge?" He looked around the circle and no one answered nor moved, but some turned to look at Roman Nose.

The rest of the leaders fell silent as they looked from the respected and almost revered Roman Nose to the accuser whose remarks smacked of an accusation of cowardice. Roman Nose was a fearsome figure of a man, standing well over six feet with a massive chest and muscular arms and legs, he was a man who had led many others into battle time and again and always emerged victorious. He was known to have killed many enemies, taken many coups, and proven himself repeatedly. He had been offered positions of leadership, even as a chief, but always refused, choosing to lead as a warrior. He glared at his accuser, nostrils flaring and eyes squinting.

"Do's White Eagle believe he is a great warrior and yet does not lead the others? I chose not to be in this charge, I have had a vision that I will be wounded and die if I do so, but I will go against this vision and I will lead our Dog Soldiers in the next attack!" He shouted his war cry, lifted his scalp-bearing war lance into the air. "Wh' will fight with Roman Nose?!"

"Most of the chiefs, war leaders and warriors around the circle jumped to their feet and shouted their war cries, knowing the history of battles fought by Roman Nose and that he was always victorious. His woman came from behind him, holding his war bonnet and held it out to her man, who turned and put it on his head, letting the long-feathered tails fall behind his back. He again shouted his war cry, screamed it loud as he lifted his lance, and swung aboard his dapple-grey stallion. With a look at the followers, he kneed his mount to a trot as he moved along and below the ridge that separated the basin from the Arikaree River.

———

THE MEN WERE busy with the dead and wounded, some had begun digging a deep depression in the middle of the island, deep enough to protect the wounded as they were brought by the others. Eli was surprised to see several of the men tending one another, thinking they should be taken to the pit where the doctor could tend them, but as he neared the gun pit where he had last seen Forsyth, he paused, watched as two men carried the doctor who had an open wound on his forehead, but still lived, and was being taken to the wounded pit.

Eli had dropped to one knee, hunkering down, for there were still some Indians in the tall grasses that were sniping at the men. He crawled closer to the gun pits where he believed Forsyth to be and saw he too had been wounded. Forsyth's head was bandaged, and his thigh showed blood and a makeshift bandage. Eli frowned as he looked at the man who appeared to be unconscious and glanced to the First Sergeant McCall. The sergeant nodded to the colonel. "He slips in an' out. We're tryin' to let him rest, he's too stubborn an' won't go back with the wounded. Reckon you need to take over, Colonel."

"You have a count of the casualties?" asked Eli.

The sergeant shook his head. "Can't, them buzzards are still snipin'. Anyone what shows his head gets shot! They been killin' the horses, but the men are usin' 'em for cover. They been diggin' like moles, never seen the like." He nodded to the next gun pit. "They shot the lieutenant right off, he's been unconscious since, ain't gonna make it. Lost too much blood, got 'im under the arm went through his chest." He looked at Eli. "Did you know that kid was the nephew o' that abolitionist preacher, Henry Ward Beecher? An' his aunt was Harriet Beecher Stowe, she's the one what wrote that book that stirred up all them northern folks, Uncle Tom's Cabin!" He shook his head again. "Just never know 'bout folks."

Eli looked at the sergeant. "You need to work your way around the island, get a casualty report. We need to know the dead, the wounded that cannot fight, and the walking wounded. Make sure the men dig their pits deep and if possible connect them. The Indians got off with the pack mules that held the medical supplies and the food, but we still have the ammunition. See if any need ammo, make a note of it and assign someone to get it to the men. Then come back here and dig another pit, there," he said, pointing to an area nearby yet behind the willows and the carcass of a dead horse.

As the sergeant moved off, crawling most of the way, Eli turned to see Forsyth stirring. He scowled at Eli. "Where's the sergeant?"

"I sent him to check the men, get a casualty report, and make sure they have ammo."

Forsyth squinted in pain. "Think they'll come again?"

"Sure as we're sittin' here. They don't give up that easy. They have us outnumbered twenty to one, but our men have keep 'em at bay and doin' one whale of a job! But…" He paused before reporting, "They got away with the mules that had the medical supplies and extra food."

Forsyth gritted his teeth as pain shot through his head, twisted around trying to get comfortable, looked at Eli. "You're a prayin' man, aren't you?"

"I am and been doin' a lot of it. You?"

"Not by nature or habit, but times like this…" He slowly shook his head and tried to look about. "We could use a lot more of it, that's for sure."

"Well, there's a good chance we won't make it outta here, so let me ask you, Colonel, if you don't make it, how's things 'tween you and God?"

"Don' know, ain't had much to do with that sort o' thing."

"Whether you've had anything to do with it or not, there comes a time when we all must stand before God and give account. That's what the Bible says, and it's best to get things right before that day, and I can help you if you want."

"Hey Colonel!" came a shout from behind Forsyth. "If'n you're gonna be prayin, include us, will ya!" It was the voice of the returning First Sergeant McCall. He had stopped and joined with George Culver to dig another gun pit.

They were hard at work behind the carcass of one of the horses, and another man called from behind him, "Better get yo' heads down, that snipin' Injun's a purty good shot!"

The words had barely been uttered then a grunt came from McCall, and a groan from Culver. The blast of the rifle in the hands of the sniping Indian that lay in the grass echoed across the narrow stream. The bullet had creased the neck of McCall and buried itself in the side of Culver's head, killing him instantly and he fell forward, hindering the digging, but McCall was more concerned about his wound. He grabbed his neckerchief, double wrapped it around his neck, tied it off and continued digging, pushing the body of Culver aside.

The thunder of hooves brought everyone's attention to the point of the island, and they peered out from the willows and over the carcasses to see a taunting Roman Nose, hurling insults at the scouts, scream his war cry and lead the charge as hundreds of shrieking warriors lay low on the necks of their mounts and charged the island. Eli turned and shouted, "Don't shoot till they hit the water!"

He looked at Forsyth, who was fading in and out of consciousness, but struggled with his pistol, readying himself for the charge. With a glance to Eli, he nodded and said, "Let's get 'em!"

CHAPTER 13

ROMAN NOSE

R oman Nose rode back and forth in front of the warriors, all screaming and shouting their war cries, working themselves up into a frenzy until Roman Nose turned to face the point of the island, lifted his war lance high, screamed and dug his heels into the ribs of his horse to lead the charge of the hundreds of warriors of the Cheyenne, Lakota, and Arapaho. They thundered toward the island, spread out in a broad front that resembled the charge of infantry, but all lay low on the necks of their mounts, still screaming and shouting.

"Here they come! Hold fire till they hit the water!" shouted Eli, turning side to side to ensure all heard the order. He lay behind a thicket of willows, parted the branches to see, and lay the muzzle of his big Spencer through the brush, searching for a target. As he watched, the leader, Roman Nose had allowed others to come close beside him and was shielded by their nearness, but Eli was determined, knowing that if the leader is killed, the others quickly lose their enthusiasm for the fight. The thunder of hooves vibrated the very ground and Eli heard the men shuffling in the gun pits, scrambling for a better firing position, but keeping out of the line of sight of the snipers in the grass.

As the horde charged, many other warriors were running through the tall grass, bent on surrounding the island and making an assault from every side, but the scouts saw the runners as easier targets and readily took aim and opened fire, cutting many of them down before they could position themselves in the grass. When the onslaught of horses splashed through the waters, they were met with the blast of more than two dozen Spencer rifles that roared, spat lead, fire and smoke, and warriors tumbled from the horses, several horses stumbled and threw their mounts, and some of the horses littered the stream alongside the painted bodies of warriors.

Without a clear shot at the leader, Eli dropped the hammer on another screaming warrior and saw him slump on the neck of his mount, but not fall. Eli quickly jacked another round into the Spencer, cocked the hammer and took a quick aim and squeezed the trigger. He was rewarded by a kick against his shoulder, the blast of the rifle, and flame, smoke and lead spat from the muzzle, carrying the message of death to another screaming warrior. As he watched, Eli saw the big leader, war bonnet flying in the wind, jerk the head of his mount around and lift his lance as he screamed to his warriors, and Eli took a steady aim as the man had his lance lifted and exposed his right side, and Eli dropped the hammer. The Spencer bucked and blasted again, and the lance of smoke and fire pointed the way for the lead projectile that flew true and blossomed red on the ribs of the big warrior. Roman Nose dropped his arm, lost his grip on the war lance, and fell on the neck of his prancing mount before sliding into the boggy grass at the river's edge.

Two warriors screamed, motioning to the fallen war leader, then both rode close beside the fallen man, lifted him between them and rode away continuing upstream to return to their camp. But the battle waged on, the mounted warriors would ride by, screaming, firing their weapons, regroup, and charge from downstream. But the word had spread about Roman Nose and the second charge was less than the first, and when they regrouped upstream, several of the warriors turned away to return to their camp, yet many remained and made one more charge.

Again, the scouts met the charge with a fusillade of lead from their Spencers and took a toll on the numbers of warriors, but more than the toll, the thought that their greatest warrior had fallen, and his medicine had failed, took the spirit out of the fight for the warriors. When the third charge passed the island, they disappeared up the gulch of the Black Wolf Creek and most of the snipers climbed the bluffs to escape the unrelenting fire from the scouts on the island.

As the battle abated, Eli looked around, called out to the gun pit on his right. "Report! Send the word around to report!"

As the word passed and the report began to return, the tally grew. "William Wilson, dead. Frank Harrington, wounded." No other report came, and Eli looked at Forsyth, who leaned forward, pistol in hand but head hanging, and asked, "You heard?"

"Yeah, not as bad as expected. Think they'll come again?"

"Dunno. When their war leader, I think it was Roman Nose, was dropped, that seemed to take the wind out of their sails. I don't think they've given up but might not see another frontal assault like the last ones. They'll probably want to retrieve their dead, after dark, but might still be some snipers."

"We need to get help, but…" Shrugged Forsyth.

Sharp Grover who was unofficially the chief of scouts and an experienced Indian fighter was in the gun pit near the colonel and heard his thought about getting help. He spoke up, "That ain't gonna happen, Colonel. Ain't no way anybody's gettin' out past those Injuns!"

Jack Stillwell, one of the youngest scouts spoke up, "If I can get someone to go with me, I'll give it a try!" From another gun pit came a raspy voice recognized by one of the old timers, Pierre Trudeau, "I'll go with ya' Jack!"

Grumbling was heard from the gun pit with Grover, "Jack's too young, ain't got much experience, he cain't get through!"

As they spoke, another man crawled near, looked over the edge of the gun pit where Forsyth and Eli sat. "Colonel, we got another'n wounded. It's Lewis Farley. He never made it to the island an' he's o'er there in the grass. He's been pickin' 'em off from there, but he's got hisself a broke leg."

"Think you can get him across after dark?" asked Forsyth.

"We can shore give it a try, Colonel. I'll see if'n I can get some help an' after dark we'll git him!"

Forsyth looked at Eli. "What'chu think about sending for help?"

"Be a good idea. I already sent Charlie Two Toes, but the more that try, the better the chance of success."

"Stillwell! Come 'ere, son. I'll make a note for you to take to the fort. You know you'll hafta make it on foot. There aren't any horses left, and if there were, you would be too easily seen."

"That's 'bout what I figgered, Colonel. But I was walkin' 'fore I was ridin', so I think we can do better afoot anyway," replied Stillwell.

"Hey, Colonel, lookee yonder!" shouted one of the men, motioning upstream where a lone warrior had appeared, sitting on his mount but holding up a white flag. He hollered in broken English, "Truce, want truce. Come talk!"

Forsyth looked at Eli. "If there's any talkin' to be done, you'll hafta do it. I can't walk on this leg."

"You want me to?" asked Eli, frowning.

"That's up to you. I don't know their lingo and wouldn't do any good anyway. I don't trust them red devils!"

"Right now, I'm not too trusting either." Eli rose and shouted, "No truce!" and was immediately answered by a shot from the grass, the bullet whipping by his head as he kicked out his feet and dropped into the pit.

———

WHEN DUSK FELL, the men began working at getting the wounded to the central pit and out of the line of fire. The count was more than earlier reported, as the total number of casualties so far was eleven plus the four dead. One of the men, Martin Burke, had decided to dig his hole a little deeper and struck water. He sent the word around and empty canteens were passed his way to be refilled and returned.

Dusk was fading when an eerie wail rolled over the hills, rising into the evening sky and rolling across the flats. It was a continuous howl, lifting and rolling, screams injected, and drums pounding. Forsyth looked at

Eli. "What is that awful racket? Is that a war dance or something?"

Eli shook his head. "No, those are women that have lost their men. They are singing the death song, wailing and weeping, it'll go on most of the night."

Forsyth shook his head, mumbled a curse and added, "Bunch o' heathens!"

Eli frowned at the man. "Didn't you say earlier that you didn't know for sure how you stood with God?"

"Yeah, but that's different. At least I believe in God!"

"They do to, in their own way, they just have different names for the one they most often call creator. But even the Bible says in James 2:19, *Thou believest in one God, thou doest well: the devils also believe and tremble.* So, tell me, Colonel, how does that make you any different?"

Forsyth frowned, grumbling something unintelligible, and said, "We'll talk about it later." He turned and sent word around the gun pits. "Cut off some of the meat from the horses, bury it in the wet sand so it'll keep a little longer."

Eli spoke softly. "Might be better to cut thin strips to hang on the brush to dry, maybe over any fire we might have to smoke." He looked to the sky and the dark-bellied clouds, shook his head, and said, "And we might be getting a rainstorm soon."

Forsyth nodded and shook his head. "Maybe that'll give us some drinkin' water." Eli passed the additional word around to find something to catch rainwater as well.

When darkness lowered its curtain of black, two men crossed the river and brought Farley into the camp, took him to the wounded pit where the men had prepared some blankets to provide a little comfort for the men. The same men went to the stack of gear and gathered the extra ammunition and worked the ranks to distribute as much as possible. They had no sooner returned to their own gun pits than the rain began to fall, but the cover of the storm was helpful to Stillwell and Trudeau as they made their getaway to go for help.

CHAPTER 14

SEARCH

Charlie Two Toes had set his sights on a rocky-faced bluff southeast of the island and before first light, after Eli had gone to his escarpment to pray and watch for an attack, Charlie knew beyond any doubt the Cheyenne and Arapaho would mount their attack soon and he chose to make his getaway and go for help. He led his buckskin gelding from the tall grass and scattered willows, waded across the shallow creek and took to the flat with the shadowy sage, bunch grass, and cholla. He moved silently and even his horse seemed to sense the need for silence and picked his footing as well. The finger ridge stood as a jagged, flat-topped point of a mesa that extended further southeast. Charlie started up the north-facing slope, picking his way in the shadowy pre-dawn darkness, still leading his horse and walking close beside the animal so their silhouettes in the pale moonlight would appear to be a lone horse.

Once atop the mesa, he saw the round-topped ridge extended farther to the southeast, and he swung aboard his mount, laying low on his neck, and nudged the gelding into a quick step trot. He guessed he had covered most of ten miles when the sun finally showed its face in the east. The bright orb was almost blinding, and Charlie took to a bit of a dry gulley to get away from making himself a blinded target easily seen in the morning light. As he traveled, he was thinking, *Most men, especially soldiers on a scout, will take the easiest way to travel, avoiding any deep river crossing, difficult terrain, or any place that could hide an ambush. Neither would they skyline themselves to make themselves an easy target for any raiding war party, nor will they want to get too far from water, so...with that in mind, I think if I make for the Republican, look it up and down, then on to Beaver River and more I'll have a better chance of running into a patrol or scout.*

What Charlie was thinking was to retrace the route taken by the scouts after leaving Fort Wallace, that if there were any troops on patrol, they would probably take the same or nearly the same route. Also, if there were any patrols from Fort Hays looking for sign of Cheyenne or Arapaho raids, they would most likely be coming this direction. He rode on into the morning, always keeping a low profile and as was his way, moving from natural cover to wooded thickets and more. Whenever a promontory offered a lookout, he would mount the bluff and have a look-see, having taken the binoculars from Eli just for that purpose.

A direct route to Fort Wallace would take a good three days, but with the continual patrols and scouts sent from the different forts that were always searching for trouble making native war parties, Charlie believed he would have a better chance of finding a patrol sooner than the three days. But his first day, from before first light to well into dusk and even by moonlight, yielded nothing. He finally chose a bit of a bluff with some piñon for cover and took to his blankets.

─────

THE LONG SHADOWS of the eastern bluffs tucked themselves away into the gulches and shoulders of the buttes and ridges, allowing the rising sun to bathe the island and bring a semblance of warmth to the weary men. The day began quietly, but all the men were watchful, fearful even, of another charge of screaming hordes wanting to take their lives and their scalps, but nothing stirred, until the sudden scream of a war cry followed by the thunder of hooves. The scouts expected to see the hordes of warriors mounting a charge, but it was a war party of no more than a dozen and the scouts were ready for them and met them with the solid blast of Spencer rifles spitting fire, smoke and lead and half the warriors tumbled off their mounts, forcing the rest to turn tail and flee. After the first charge, only random snipers fired from the tall grass, keeping everyone alert and anxious. But the day passed with nothing more than the grass-crawling shooters who seldom made a hit, none killing any scouts.

Their own rations gone, the men began to subsist on strips of dried horsemeat, but that did not last long, and they knew they would have to resort to the meat buried in the sand which had already started rotting. The stench of dead horses and men was made all the worse with the blistering sun that shone bright from the brassy sky and all hope of any more rain perished with the clear sky and nothing resembling a cloud. The men kept busy digging trenches between gun pits, yet never exerting themselves due to the scarcity of food but digging was better than worrying. Scout C.B. Nichols, frustrated as were the others, stood, shaking his hand overhead, and hollered at the hillsides.

"Why don't you red devils come on an' get it o'er with? I'm tired o' waitin' and I wanna kill me some Injuns!"

Before he said another word, a bullet whispered past his ear, the blast of the rifle following, and he did a dive into the muddy bottom of his pit and never said another word.

And so it continued for another day and when dusk dropped its curtain, the colonel summoned most of the men near, and when they assembled, he struggled to face the men, he grimaced, looked at the men, and began "Men, there's no sense in me tryin' to tell you something you already know, but I think we need to try to send out another scout or two to go for help. We don't know if Stillwell and Trudeau made it, and there's no sense waiting for help that might not be coming."

The men looked around at one another until John Donovan looked at his pit partner, Allison Pliley, then back to the colonel. "We'll go, Colonel. Ain't nuthin' out there any worse'n what's happenin' here!"

"Alright. Then you need to head straight for Fort Wallace, it's about seventy-five miles, and will take you most of five days, but have them come straight on here." He then lowered his voice and added what most were thinking. "Hopefully there'll still be some of us left," stated Forsyth.

The two volunteers waited until full dark before sneaking out, crawling through the shallow water and into the tall grass, one close behind the other, making their progress slow and quiet, so much so that one of the men asked the colonel in a whispered voice, "Ain't Donovan and Pliley goin'?"

"They're already gone!" answered the colonel, struggling after taking another bullet, this one shattering his lower leg and rendering him unable to move.

Using the light of the moon, he used his razor and worked to cut out the bullet from the festering wound in his leg, and soon had the ball freed and tossed aside, rebinding the wound. But the volunteers disappeared and made their getaway in silence and apparently unobserved as there were no gunshots nor screamed war cries or anything else that would tell of discovery.

Two more days passed, and the men ate the last of their dried meat and anything else they could scavenge. Three men volunteered to leave the island and try to find some game, but all they found was a prairie dog village with a bunch of whistle pigs that would not come out of their dens and the men returned empty-handed.

The sniping by the natives had stopped, and it appeared they had decided they would just lay siege and starve out the scouts. But it was soon evident they had given up even on the siege and were leaving. After the fall of darkness on the sixth day, with the rations gone, meat spoiled, and nothing to eat, some tried putting gunpowder on the meat to make it palatable, but even that failed.

So the men began doing what men have done since before time was recorded, they began grumbling and griping until one suggested, "Mebbe the rest of us that ain't injured oughta just strike out on our own and try to get back to the fort."

When the complaining and suggestion to leave reached the colonel, he called the men together and spoke. "Men, I know how you feel. We're all hungry, tired, mad and frustrated beyond anything any of us ever experienced before, but…" He paused, looking from man to man. "I expect every man to live up to his word when you said you would fight to the end. Now, I'm asking you to stick it out, at least until the men we've sent for relief have time to make it back. And besides that, our friends and comrades that can't leave, well…" He paused again. "I believe it to be our duty, as friends and men, to stick together. But when the time comes and no relief shows, then I have no further claim on you, and you may do whatever you think best to save your own lives." He looked around the circle at all the men whose heads hung, and nothing was said until John Hurst spoke up and said, "Colonel, we'll never desert the wounded, no matter what happens, we stay with them and die with 'em if'n we have to!"

By the eighth day, the men had lost most of their strength and some lost even the will to live, but they still managed to hang on, even though it appeared all hope was gone. They calculated how long it would take men on foot to reach Fort Wallace, decided it to be four to five days, at most, six days and relief should only take three to four days. They had been on the island for eight days, and that day was soon passing with the hot sun overhead and nothing but rotten meat and muddy water to try to last another day.

CHAPTER 15

HOPE

C harlie Two Toes mounted the rocky face of the round knobbed butte, binoculars in hand, hope high but waning and bellied down to search the flats for another day. He had crossed the two forks of Beaver River and earlier today had crossed the Middle Fork of Sappa Creek. Now he was on a bluff overlooking the swale of the South Fork of Sappa Creek. He guessed he had come close to seventy miles and was getting anxious to find help. He lifted the binoculars to scan the low valley of the creek and the rolling grassy plains beyond. Below the butte, the grey snags of dead cottonwoods stood with bare limbs scratching for the blue of the hot sky, appearing as long dead and desperate skeletons that warned of any travelers that dared enter this empty land. The little water in the creek appeared, struggled through a grassy bog and resurfaced some distance to the southwest.

As he slowly searched the rolling flats before him, he carefully moved the binoculars from the north in a wide arc to the south, but nothing moved until he saw a small bunch of pronghorn antelope that lifted their heads in alarm at something they saw. Charlie moved the binoculars in the direction of the antelopes' stare and thought he saw a bit of dust. He lowered the binoculars, squinted to look with shaded eyes, then lifted the binoculars again. As he watched, a long line of dusty blue showed itself to be a troop of cavalry, plodding along, making a straight ride to the west-northwest. If he stayed where he was, they would pass not too far away, but Charlie was tired of waiting and hurriedly returned to his mount, cased the binoculars, and took off at a steady lope toward the cavalry.

As he neared, he took off his hat and waved to get their attention. The troops halted, and their commander, Captain Louis Carpenter, sat waiting for the rider to near. As Charlie reined up, the captain frowned and said, "You're an Indian!"

Charlie grinned, looking at the captain, whose stern expression made Charlie grimace. The captain, who had been a lieutenant colonel in the war, had a handlebar mustache with a snippet of whiskers under his lower lip. The image made Charlie think the man had swallowed a longhorn steer, tail first, and he could not help grinning.

He answered the question as to his native appearance. "Not so's you'd notice," as he was dressed as the other scouts in a combination of buckskins, linen shirt, leather vest, felt hat. "I'm Charlie Two Toes, scout with Colonel Forsyth's Scouts! I've come for help."

"Help?" asked the captain.

"The entire company of scouts are pinned down on an island in the Arikaree, there's about five or six hundred Cheyenne, Arapaho, and Lakota, maybe even some Kiowa, that are doin' their best to wipe 'em out. But when I left, they were holdin' their own."

"Did Forsyth send you?"

"No sir, his second in command, Colonel Elijah McCain, sent me. They are out of rations, lost most of their horses, probably all of 'em by now, and they need relief!" declared a desperate Charlie.

"How'd you find us?" asked the colonel, frowning and a little skeptical that this native was giving this report.

"I've been scoutin' for the last two and a half days. Thought it would be quicker to find a patrol than to go all the way to Wallace or Hays."

"And how do we know you're not one of the natives leading us into a trap?"

Charlie shook his head. "I'm Pawnee! My people have been fighting the Cheyenne and Arapaho since long before any settlers came into this land. Besides, I was with Colonel McCain when he delivered that horse you're riding to Fort Hays. We drove that herd all the way from California!"

The colonel was finally convinced for he was well aware of the recent purchase of remounts that came from California and those were details that the natives would not know. He looked at Charlie. "I'm Captain Louis Carpenter, commanding Troops H & I of the Tenth Cavalry Regiment." And with a wave and a signal to the troops, he looked at Charlie. "Scout Charlie Two Toes, lead the way!"

Charlie had recognized this was a detachment of Buffalo Soldiers and he was happy for it, for it was Buffalo Soldiers, Company F of the Tenth, that had helped out the drovers of the herd from California at the Saline River. He grinned and started back toward the Arikaree and Forsyth's Scouts.

———

IT WAS late on the third day for the Tenth, but the eighth day on the island for the scouts, when one of the men shouted, "Hey Colonel, look yonder! Ain't that our troops!" As one man, the entire party of survivors stood to look to the downstream end of the island to see the banner of the Tenth Cavalry and the red, white, and blue of the American flag whipping in the breeze. The dusty riders that carried the banners looked tired and trailworn, but to the men on the island, they looked like angels dressed in dusty blue.

One of the riders kicked his mount into a lope and came charging into the stream, splashing water far and wide as he shouted, "Hey scouts! It's me, Donovan!"

Cheers greeted the man who had left the island with Al Pliley about six days ago and who they had little hope for, but as he dropped to the ground and some of the men were shaking his hand and slapping him on the shoulder, they said, "Boy, yore a sight for sore eyes! You got anything to eat?"

Donovan frowned and looked around. "What'd you do, kill 'em all?"

"Nah, they just gave up and left!" came the answer.

Donovan chuckled. "There's lots to eat with the troops, they'll get ever'body moved off this stinkin' island."

"Wal, we're sure glad you made it!" answered Grover.

Donovan shook his head. "We just run into 'em on the way back. I recruited four others to start back, but Charlie Two Toes already had the troops headin' thisaway."

Eli had joined the men at the greeting party and asked, "Where is Charlie?"

"Aw, he's back there with them Buffalo Soldiers.

They'll be settin' up some tents an' such to move you fellas back away from this stinkin' place."

———

IT WAS another five days before the relief column and the rescued scouts returned to Fort Wallace, but Eli and Charlie left the island bound for Fort Hays. He was to report to General Sheridan, and it was a good week after leaving the island when Eli and Charlie rode into the grounds of Fort Hays. They were weary, dirty, and hungry, but Eli followed protocol and while Charlie took the horses and gear to the stables, he reported to General Sheridan.

"That's right general, Forsyth's Scouts proved themselves to be exceptional. Even after taking three bullets, hardly able to move, Forsyth did a good job of keeping the men in order, defending the island, saving lives. But, like I already said, none of it would have happened if he hadn't been looking for a fight and took us beyond the range of our supplies. But that's just my opinion, and that's about all it's worth."

"So, he didn't do anything wrong, like break regulations or anything, he just didn't show good judgment?"

Eli grinned and nodded. "And that's something every officer has done at one time or another. But"—he took a heavy sigh—"if it's all the same to you, if I'm gonna scout, I'd rather it be with some other outfit."

"So be it. I'm recalling Colonel Custer to take over the Seventh Cavalry and as soon as he gets settled in, he'll be leavin' on another huntin' trip, huntin' war parties of the Cheyenne, and he'll need a good scout so you an' Charlie could go with him. But that'll be a while yet, so once you get recuperated, I'll have you and

Charlie doin' some independent scoutin' and gettin' me a better idea of what the Indians are doing."

Eli nodded, grinned, slowly stood, and said, "As long as we're not leavin' in the morning. I need a bath, some good food, and about two or three days of sleep."

"You'll be in the barracks?"

"Either there or the stables, depends on where we find the best company." Eli grinned as he turned to leave.

Chapter 16

Questions

For three days, Eli and Charlie loafed around the post, most of their time spent in the barracks cleaning their weapons, repairing their gear and getting some much-needed rest. On the fourth day, they went to the stables to take care of their horses and while some of the troops on discipline shoveled the manure from the stalls, Eli and Charlie groomed their horses. Both men were skilled at horseshoeing and all the horses were needing new shoes so while Eli pulled off the old ones, Charlie worked at the forge and anvil fitting new shoes for the three horses.

As they worked, First Sergeant Bill McCall came into the stable, saw the two working and began talking, sharing the experience on the island that Forsyth had dubbed as Beecher Island, after his executive officer, Lieutenant Beecher. "So, you two gettin' all rested up and filled up after our little excursion?" asked McCall, grinning at the two men.

Eli chuckled. "I don't think I'll ever get filled up after that! Sometimes just thinkin' about that stinkin' meat and muddy water, I get hungry for real food. Then I get to thinkin' I'm still so hungry, it seems like my belly button is pinchin' my backbone!"

Sergeant McCall chuckled too. "I know what you mean. After that stinkin' horse meat, I even had a hard time cuttin' into the beef steak Cooky fixed for me. But… it didn't take me too long to get over it, and I even had Cooky fix me another'n." He laughed. "And I used to think the coffee in the chow hall was a sorry imitation for real coffee, but you know what, that first pot I drunk all by myself and it shore tasted good!"

"Was that here or down at Wallace?" asked Charlie.

"Wal, while you two cut out for hereabouts, we'ns went to Wallace. That was right after Farley died an' we buried him on the island with the others. Then when we got to Wallace, O'Donnell died, buried him at the fort."

The somber news cast a pall over their conversation and the men worked in silence until the sergeant stepped to the gate of the stall where Eli was finishing up with brushing Rusty and McCall leaned on the top rail to watch. With a glance about to see if anyone else was near, the sergeant spoke softly as he asked, "Eli, when we was on the island, before that last big charge, you asked the colonel 'bout how things were 'tween him an' God. I was listenin' and you never got to finish what you was talkin' 'bout." He paused as Eli straightened up, tossed the brush into the rack beside the hay mow, and walked closer to the sergeant. "An' I was wonderin', you know, cuz after that little episode, I been thinkin' 'bout muh own self and what would happen were I to take one o' them arrows in *my* chest an' not make it outta there. And it's kinda got me concerned, you know? I ain't been the best man around, done me a lot o' wrong, kilt men in the war, kilt some red men, and well…" He shrugged, looking a little shamefaced.

Eli grabbed his Bible from the stack of gear in the corner and pushed through the gate of the stall, and motioned for the sergeant to join him as he walked nearer the big door for the light to look about. They took a seat near one another on a couple of benches and Eli began. "Sarge, there's a lotta folks have the wrong idea about gettin' to Heaven, most seem to think that if our good works outweigh our bad ones, then the scales are in our favor, and we'll make it." He began flipping through the pages of the Bible and stopped, looked up at the sergeant. "But the Bible tells us in Ephesians 2:8-9 *For by grace are ye saved through faith; and that not of yourselves: it is the gift of God: Not of works, lest any man should boast.* See, Sarge, when it says being saved is a gift, not of works, lest any man should boast. If it was based on the good that we do, when we get to Heaven, there would be people struttin' around braggin' about what they did and what others didn't, that's what it means *lest any man should boast.* And God doesn't want that, that's why He says being saved is through believing on Him and receiving the gift of salvation."

The sergeant smiled and nodded. "So, if it's a gift, anybody can get it?"

"Well, yeah, but…" began Eli, and the sergeant said, "I knew it was too good to be true!" he grumbled, shaking his head.

"Whoa, wait a minute. Let me explain, it is a gift, and anybody can get it, but it's not like just grabbing a package off the table. It's easy enough though. See, He explains it a little better over here in the book of Romans." He flipped some pages, looking for the passage and stopped, pointed his finger to the page. "Here's what you need to know, here in 3:23 *For all have sinned, and come short of the glory of God."*

"That's me alright," grumbled the crusty old sergeant.

"That's the first thing we need to know is that we're, both you and me, are all sinners and because of that, we don't measure up to God's standard. But..." Eli grinned as he flipped a couple more pages. "See here, in 6:23, *For the wages of sin is death...*because we're sinners, we're doomed to death, and that's not just dying and going to the grave, that's goin' to hell forever!" emphasized Eli, looking at a startled sergeant, who leaned back, wide-eyed as he looked at Eli.

Eli chuckled. "But the best part...*but the gift of God is eternal life through Jesus Christ our Lord.* There it is—the gift of God, and like any other gift, you must believe in it and accept it. Understand that, Sergeant?"

"I think so, I believe it, but how do I accept it?"

Eli grinned. "That's easy, look here." He flipped a couple pages and pointed to 10:9. *"That if thou shalt confess with thy mouth the Lord Jesus, and shalt believe in thine heart that God hath raised him from the dead, thou shalt be saved.* And down in verse 13 *For whosoever shall call upon the name of the Lord shall be saved.* Remember where we started, it said *for by grace are ye saved through faith* that's what it means, faith is just believing God and His word, and if you believe what I've shown you here in His word, remember it said, *believe in thine heart* then all you have to do is call upon Him, and we do that in prayer, and ask for that gift to be saved and have eternal life, then it's yours."

The sergeant let a slow smile paint his face as he pondered what he had learned, then leaned forward and asked, "Really? That's all there is to it?"

"It's more than you think, Sarge, remember it said *believe in thine heart* that's not just trying something out just in case, or getting a ticket to stick in your pocket, it's a deep down in your heart belief and acceptance of what His word says and what Jesus has done for us. The penalty for our sin is death and hell forever, but Jesus went to the cross to pay that penalty for us and by doing that, he provides that gift of salvation and eternal life for us. Do you believe that?"

"Oh you betcha! That there's the best news I ever heard in muh whole life!" declared the sergeant, then he frowned. "Can…can I get that gift now?"

Eli grinned. "Sure, Sarge. Let's just pray together and ask for that gift." He bowed his head and was followed by the sergeant. Eli led in prayer and asked God to guide the sergeant as he confessed he was a sinner, and to accept the gift of eternal life. The sergeant repeated the prayer, and when they said "Amen" he looked at Eli, had tears in his eyes as he reached out to shake Eli's hand and said, "Thanks, Eli, thanks."

The sergeant stood, a broad smile on his face and started from the stables, stopped and turned back to look at Eli, grinned and with a wave. "Thanks again!" he said and turned away to go to the chow hall.

Eli watched as he left, a smile on his face as well, as he said a silent prayer of thanksgiving for the sergeant's decision but was interrupted when he heard the voice of Charlie, who had been watching and listening.

"So, does that apply to me? Seein' as how I'm one o' them heathen redskins?" He grinned.

"Of course it does, Charlie! Did you say that same prayer with us, you know, about confessing you're a sinner and asking God to forgive you and to give you that free gift of eternal life?"

Charlie grinned, dropped his eyes and mumbled, "Yeah, reckon I did!"

"Charlie, that's great! You'll find that what you've done is the greatest thing ever. Might take a while for it all to sink in, but…" He shrugged, stood and went to his friend, shook hands, and added, "I'm happy for you, Charlie."

Charlie, still with his head lowered, mumbled, "After he talked about bein' a bad man an' such, and wonderin' 'bout Heaven, I kinda started payin' attention. Heard it all, glad I did, now I know!" He grinned as he lifted his eyes to Eli. The two men shook hands, brought one another close and slapped their shoulders with the free hand, both men grinning broadly.

"Now, can we go get somethin' to eat?" asked Charlie.

"Of course, then I'll hafta go see the general. I think he's got somethin' he wants us to do."

CHAPTER 17

SOUTH

"I've got letters here," began a frustrated General Sheridan, shuffling papers on his desk as he stood behind the bureau. "From John Evans, the former governor of Colorado territory, from Nehemiah Green, governor of Kansas, Alexander Hunt, the current governor of Colorado and the ex officio Superintendent of Indian Affairs, all of 'em wantin' me to do somethin' 'bout these consarned Indian raids that are killing settlers, scaring the daylights outta would-be settlers, and aggravating the communities all across the plains!"

He plopped down in the chair behind the desk, leaned back and jerked forward to extend his arms across the top of the desk, clenched his fists. "I'm tellin' ya' Eli, it gets me Irish dander up!" He shook his head and looked directly at Eli. "And what's frustratin' me more'n anything else is, I don't know what they're doin'!" He slammed his fist on the desktop to emphasize his concern. "That's what I want you an' Charlie to do. I want you two to head out in the morning, go south to Fort Larned, then on to Fort Cobb. All the way, I want you looking for Indians, Cheyenne, Arapaho, Lakota, Kiowa, Kiowa Apache, all of 'em! And I want to know what they're doin' and if you can figger it out, I wanna know what they're goin' to do!"

He leaned back in his chair, and the man known as Little Phil, softened a bit and looked at Eli. "I need somebody I can trust, and that's you. I remember in the war, while other officers, including me, were doin' their best to climb the ranks, you just wanted to do your job and let tomorrow take care of itself. I like that. Now"—he paused and pulled out a sheath of papers—"after the signing of this treaty, they call it the Medicine Lodge Treaty, the Cheyenne and Arapaho are supposed to be on the reservation in Indian Territory, but I've been getting reports about the raids like what you've experienced. Now I know, the chief of the Cheyenne, Black Kettle, has said he wants peace, but the worst ones that have been doin' the raiding are the Dog Soldiers of Tall Bull of the Cheyenne and some of the other young bucks, and they're not the only ones."

"And what do you plan to do about 'em, General?" asked Eli, a little suspicious of his assignment.

"Dunno, and I won't know till I get your report. That's why you need to go—I want as accurate and detailed report as possible. I'll have to put it alongside the other reports I always get from other posts and such, then we'll see if we can come up with some kind of master plan and bring this constant raiding and such to an end."

"I know it's impossible, but if you could get the politicians in Washington to ratify and honor some of these treaties, you know, the old-fashioned thing, keep your word, then maybe the natives wouldn't be so cantankerous. The way I understand it, General, that treaty"—nodding his head to the Medicine Lodge Treaty the general had mentioned that lay on his desk—"the Cheyenne were supposed to have the right to follow the buffalo north for their spring and fall hunts, but every time they cross the Arkansas River, problems between the settlers, troopers, and others break out and somebody ends up dead, when all they wanted to do was hunt buffalo."

"I know, I know, but the final draft of the treaty did not include that right. They're supposed to stay south and go to their reservation."

Eli shook his head. "See there, the natives can't trust the white men to keep their word."

"Well, neither one of us can do anything about that now. All I want to do is prevent more settlers getting killed or freighters crossing the Santa Fe Trail getting slaughtered." He slapped his open palm on the desk, scattering some of the papers.

Eli grinned, stood and extended his hand to shake. "We'll leave at first light, General."

The general stood, extended his hand, and grinned. "I knew I could count on you!"

———

ELI AND CHARLIE left the fort when the eastern horizon was a vague shadow below the canopy of dusty blue that faded to black above their shoulder height. The horses had rested for several days and were glad to be back on the trail. Eli aboard his big claybank stallion, trailing the dapple-grey mustang as the packhorse, and Charlie aboard his buckskin gelding. The horses stretched out, setting a good pace for the cool of the morning. The beginning of October in the plains was blanketed by cool air and the hardwood trees of the riparian forests were already shedding their fall colors. What just days or weeks before had been brilliant hues of gold, orange, red and more, had now faded to dim colors, most showing dusky shades of brown and dusty gold. The slightest breeze cut the leaves from their tenuous grip and let them flutter to the ground to blanket the ground to absorb and hold the moisture of the coming winter.

The sky was mostly clear and as the canopy of darkness retreated to the west and the pale blues gave way to the orange-tinted clouds that still hugged the eastern flats, the clouds soon dissipated and surrendered to the coming warmth of the rising sun. Charlie turned to face the blazing orb and lifted his hands high, closed his eyes, and absorbed the first rays of the day.

Eli watched and chuckled. "You act like you never saw a sunrise before!"

"This is the first time I saw the sunrise today! And every sunrise is a gift from the creator!" answered a very somber Charlie, until he let the grin slowly split his face and give a sparkle of mischief to his eyes.

They came to the Smoky Hill River about an hour after first light, turned east to follow it downstream below the confluence with Big Timber creek and cut into the trees and made their crossing, continuing to the south. The flatlands stretched out before them, the tall grasses moving like the waves of the ocean, their fall colors showing tawny shades from dusty pale tans to deep reds and the Indian grass showing a few leftover purple flowers.

It was a peaceful sight, soothing almost, with the gentle wave that tended toward mesmerizing to the lone riders, until Charlie called out, "There!" pointing to a break in the waves that showed a trail of flattened grass that had been trampled under the hooves of many riders.

The two men moved closer, and both dropped to the ground to give the trail a better look. Charlie stood, looking in the way of the tracks to get a better understanding of the direction of their travel. "Looks to be ten, maybe fifteen, movin' northwest. I'm thinkin' young bucks wantin' to get some game or scalps." He turned to look down the back trail, shaded his eyes from the rising sun and said, "They're travelin' in a straight line, they know where they're goin'."

"They could be goin' to join with the Dog Soldiers, and could be Cheyenne, Arapaho, Kiowa, even Comanche," surmised Eli, still staring at the tracks. He lifted his head, looking both up trail and back, walked a little ways to the northwest following the sign, but seeing nothing unusual or different, stepped back aboard his horse and nodded to Charlie. "Let's keep goin'."

By noon, they had crossed another trail of what they presumed was that of either a war party or hunting party and since the buffalo had already migrated south, they could only assume this was another band of young bucks bent on raiding and killing settlers. As they took their nooning, Charlie said, "I'm thinkin' we should split up, one east, one west. Both those trails came from almost due south, but Sheridan was wantin' sign of villages goin' to the reservation, and so far…" He shrugged.

"I think you're right, but if we split up, do we meet up again or just keep wanderin' around?" asked Eli, knowing they would cover more territory, but it would be more dangerous traveling alone and they needed to coordinate their search to provide a better understanding for Sheridan.

"Due south, 'bout four, five miles is Sand Creek, and

another three, four south of that is Walnut Creek. There's another creek that comes in from the south and I think some folks call it Otter Creek, but if you go southeast and hit the second creek, come back upstream to that confluence and we'll meet there. I'll do the same to the west, meet you there. That'll be 'bout dusk for the both of us. That way, we'll cover more country, maybe find more trails."

Eli pondered what Charlie suggested and nodded. "We'll do it. But try your best to stay outta trouble. I don't want to hafta come lookin' for you after dark, there ain't gonna be much moonlight!" chuckled Eli as he rose to climb aboard his big claybank. The men waved to one another and started in their opposite directions, watching the grasses and the breeze for the first sign of passing bands.

Mid-afternoon, Eli spotted a lone rider coming from the south and crossing Sand Creek. Eli reined up, slipped his binoculars from the saddlebags and had a good look, readily recognizing the man as a white man that looked like he could be a scout. Eli cased the field glasses and sat, watching him come near. As he closed the distance, Eli lifted a hand to wave and the man nodded, nudging his horse in Eli's direction. "Howdy! You looked to be comin' from the southeast, any Indian trouble?" asked Eli.

"Nope, no trouble. Seen a bunch, but no trouble," answered the man. "But I got 'nuff sense to make myself scarce whenever there's natives around. You?"

"Sign, but nothin' else." He paused, then added, "I'm Eli McCain, scoutin' outta Hays, You?"

"Craig, Henry Craig, scoutin' outta Fort Cobb."

Both men sat, forearms crossed over the pommels of their saddles and leaning forward. Eli pushed his hat back and asked, "So, Sheridan sent us down thisaway, stop at Larned, mebbe go on to Cobb, swing back around and report. But if you could tell me 'bout what's happenin' down thataway, you'd save us some miles."

"Us?" he asked, looking around.

"Got a partner. We split up, goin' to meet up down to Walnut Creek."

"If'n you got coffee an' anything to go with it, we might just share a camp, if'n that'd be alright."

"Sure, let's talk as we ride," agreed Eli.

They turned south and crossed Dry Creek, moved through the woods and into the open grassland and Craig began to tell Eli, "Down to Cobb, them Kiowas, ol' Satanta, Lone Wolf and Black Eagle all have their camps 'round 'bout Fort Cobb, reckon they like bein' close to the food. There's other camps along the Washita of Comanche and Kiowa Apache, and I'm to scout out upstream of the Washita to see what other camps I find."

"How many natives you reckon in those camps around Cobb?" asked Eli.

"Oh, I'd guess som'eres 'bout twenty-five hundred or maybe more."

"That'll be their winter camp?"

"Ummhmm, but from what I've seen before, there'll be a whole lot more upstream from there. I made a big loop goin' northeast, past Fort Larned, then swingin' around to the west and come mornin' will be headin' south an' down to the Washita then back to Cobb."

"If it's alright with you, we'd like to check out the Washita with you."

"Suits me, I could stand the comp'ny, and you've got coffee!" he grinned.

CHAPTER 18

ARKANSAS

"You seem to know the different people pretty well, been scoutin' 'em a while?" asked Charlie. The three men were sitting around the campfire, enjoying the last of the coffee before they turned in for the night.

"Should most of 'em come into Cobb to get their rations and such or to the tradin' post to see Dutch Bill. He's got him a Cheyenne wife, or had, she died just 'fore I left. She was from Black Kettle's band of Cheyenne, got consumption. Ol' Bill was purty sad 'bout it, had to send word to her people 'bout her dyin'. Said he was gonna urge Black Kettle to come into the fort an' talk with Colonel Hazen 'bout makin' peace. Said he was hopin' Black Kettle would get some o' the other chiefs, Little Robe of the Cheyenne, Spotted Wolf and Big Mouth of the Arapaho, mebbe some others, to come with him and make peace for the winter," explained Henry Craig.

"Ever'body's willin' to talk peace, even make up a treaty, but so far, ain't seen many of 'em keep those treaties, white men or red," grumbled Charlie.

Eli looked at Charlie over his coffee cup that was still steaming, the steam catching the light from the fire. "Tell me 'bout the sign you saw on your scout this afternoon."

Charlie nodded, sipped his coffee and looked at Eli over the fire. "Wide trail, many travois, horses, I'd guess mebbe a couple hunnert people, and the trail was at least a week old. Came from the northwest, headin' south, southeast. I'm guessin' to the Washita."

"Any idea who?"

"Prob'ly Arapaho, dunno for sure."

"That'd be 'bout right, comin' from thataway. Most of the Southern Cheyenne are already south of us, they usually make their winter camp on the Washita," offered Henry.

The three men continued to talk into the night as most lonely men are wont to do, but they were always watchful, careful to keep an eye on their horses for the animals would sense something before the men would hear or see anything. They split the watch, with Charlie taking first watch, Henry the second and Eli the last watch. But it was a peaceful night and morning came all too soon.

With a cup of coffee and a handful of jerky for breakfast, the three scouts took to the trail before the sun showed its face, but they enjoyed the colors of early morning off their left shoulders as they picked their way through the tall grasses of the flatlands. By time for nooning, they had crossed the Pawnee River, saw smoke in the trees south and upon discovering the noon camp of a cavalry troop, they hailed the camp and took their noon meal with the troop.

"I'm Captain Nicholas Nolan, Commander of Company A, Tenth Cavalry, Fort Larned," stated the commander as he extended his hand first to Eli and then to the others. Nolan was a hatchet-faced man with a long drooping mustache but with a sparkle in his eyes and a bit of a grin showing at all times. He motioned for the three visitors to be seated and after the cook passed a plate of beans and pork belly along with a cup of steaming coffee to each man, the captain asked, "So, you're all scouts but from different posts?"

Henry answered, "That's right, Captain, I'm from Fort Cobb, met up with these two last night." He grinned as he attacked his beans with vigor.

"And I'm Elijah McCain, and this is Charlie Two Toes. @e're out of Fort Hays, under the command of General Sheridan."

The captain looked at Eli. "You look to be a former officer, am I right?"

Eli grinned. "Lieutenant Colonel under Sheridan at Appamatox."

"Thought so, the name was familiar. So, what's brought you men into this area?"

Eli glanced at the others, then to the captain. "Sheridan's getting pressure to do something about the raids and such, so we're scouting to see what's goin' on and where."

The captain nodded, frowned, and began. "We just had a little confrontation with some Kiowa and Comanche that raided a couple freighters near Fort Dodge, we chased 'em a few miles to Mulberry Creek, kilt three of 'em, wounded some more, but they were done and high-tailed it south. Last month, there were sixteen settlers an' freighters killed on the Pawnee, west of Fort Larned." He shook his head, remembering. "General Sully had ordered the agent, Wynkoop, to not give the Cheyenne any more arms, but the agent thought the general was wrong, believed 'none of my natives would deceive me,' and gave in to their demands for weapons so they could hunt and would not starve. They're the ones that have been raidin' on the Saline and Solomon. Last word was they killed sixteen farmers and done some women wrong." He shook his head and sipped some coffee. "Last I heard, Wynkoop was relieved of his job, and rightly so. Major Asbury is also gone, now we have Captain Dangerfield Parker, commanding."

"Well, we were supposed to stop by Larned to get a report, but we thought we'd go on to the Washita, try to find out who all is there and what might be happening."

"Is it true what we heard, that Sheridan is planning a winter campaign against the natives?" asked the curious captain.

"Well, since he doesn't confide in me, I don't know what he's planning, but he's been getting pressure from the governors, freighters, settlers and more," answered Eli, standing and tossing out the dregs of his coffee and turning in the plate and cup to the cook. The others followed his lead and after thanking the captain, the three scouts resumed their journey south.

As the sun began to tuck itself away beneath the golden curtain in the west, the three scouts had crossed Coon Creek and were crossing the Arkansas River. The cottonwoods stubbornly clung to the last of the browning leaves that fluttered in the breeze, the silver maple had shed theirs and the oak and hackberry still held their leaves, although fading in color. A clearing among the almost naked skeletons of trees that had afforded shade in the summer, now beckoned with a carpet of newly shed leaves and the men prepared to make camp for the night. The breeze was cool as dusk

lowered and captured the remaining light and held it
close, a meadowlark trilled its call, and a late harvesting
squirrel scolded the intruders. Charlie gathered some
wood for a fire while Eli stripped his horses. Stacking the
packs at the base of a nearby hackberry, he gave his and
Charlie's horses a rubdown while Charlie set about
making supper. Henry had volunteered to climb a big bur
oak and with binoculars in hand, get a better look at
their surroundings. With scattered trees, tall grasses, dry
land with sage, greasewood, and more, there were many
places that could hide a raiding party of natives and none
of the men were willing to get careless in this country.

After leaving the company of the Tenth Cavalry,
Charlie had bagged a big turkey and had it hanging over
the fire, its juices sizzling in the low flames, and a dutch
oven sat on a bed of coals baking some cornmeal
biscuits. When all was ready, the men enjoyed the feast
and Charlie looked up, frowning. "Say, ain't it close to
Thanksgiving time?"

"Thanksgiving? You mean that holiday that Washington declared about a hunnert years ago?" asked a
grinning Henry.

"It ain't no special day, just whenever the president
says it should be," clarified Eli.

"Then, *I* declare it to be a holiday!" announced Charlie, a smug smile splitting his face as he pulled a leg off
the tender turkey.

They enjoyed the feast, leaving few scraps for the
scavengers, and turned in early, agreeing to keep a vigilant watch continuous for the night. Henry had seen
nothing that would be of concern when he climbed up in
the tree before supper, but none of the three men were
comfortable, especially after the reports from the men of

the Tenth and the different fights going on in the western half of the state.

It was just a sliver of moon that hung in the south-west darkness, the dark line of horizon showing in the west under the pale sky where the lanterns of the night still hung above the scratchy horizon that showed skeletal fingers of leafless trees as silhouettes. Eli had relieved Henry and would stand watch until first light and as always, he began the shift with a time of quiet conversation with his Lord. As he whispered his prayer, he continually moved, keeping himself in the darkest shadows of the trees, and always watching the horses for any sign of alarm.

The eastern horizon was just beginning to reveal itself, when Rusty's head came up and his nostrils flared as he looked to the flats south of the tree line. The grey also lifted his head as did the buckskin and the bay of Henry. Low rumbles came from the chest of Rusty and Eli knew there was something threatening south of their camp. Standing close beside a big cottonwood, Eli searched the rolling flats, tall grasses waving in the early morning breeze, but when he saw where some of the grass was not moving like the rest, the waves had parted, he knew someone, or something was approaching the camp. Eli bent down, picked up a small stone, and tossed it to Charlie, waking him instantly. Charlie did not move, but slowly turned his head to look to Eli, and with a simple signal, Charlie recognized there was danger, quickly came from his blankets, reached to awaken Henry, but he was also coming from his blankets and the two men joined Eli.

With a nod in the direction of the stilted movements, the three began to search the entire area before the camp, knowing that seldom do attacks come from just one direction. Charlie and Henry moved away from Eli, using the trees for cover, knowing they were in the darkness with the trees behind them, but the low glow of the cookfire would keep the attention of any attackers.

Expecting close-up action, Eli held his Colt revolver shotgun, never taking his eyes off the movement in the grass. As he watched, he could almost hear his own heart beating more rapidly, his breathing was shallow and rapid, and he forced himself to relax, lean against the tree and slowly lift the shotgun.

Even though expected, the charge came suddenly as several warriors jumped from the grass, screaming their war cries, two shooting their rifles, but their charge was met with the instant firing of three weapons. Charlie and Henry both had Spencer repeaters and the heavy blast of those two .52 caliber rifles bracketed the boom of Eli's shotgun. But the screams of war cries suddenly changed to cries of terror and wounds as three warriors were blasted off their feet and others were startled at the sudden response to what they thought would be a terrifying charge. The leader had been taken by the full blast from Eli's shotgun and was lifted off his feet to fall in a clump on his back, his middle almost obliterated by the pellet impacts. And it was terrifying, but not for the scouts, the young warriors of both the Kiowa and Cheyenne, felt the second blast from the three white men, all experienced Indian fighters, and the sudden charge was also suddenly stopped as six bodies lay in the grass and the rest of the warriors disappeared into the darkness that seems darker just before the coming of light. Moans came from two of the attackers, and Charlie and Henry sought them out, giving each a coup de grâce.

Silence fell over the camp as each man stood in the

fading darkness, looking about, searching for any additional attackers or threat, but none came. When the squirrel began to scold the three for waking him up and disturbing his solitude, they grinned, turned back to their camp to make ready for the day's journey.

CHAPTER 19

WASHITA

As the three men rode together, always southward, they talked. It was the way of wandering men to learn about the country they were in and going to, seeking to pry as much information from those that had traveled this way before, making mental maps of the unfamiliar land, a map that could be brought out and examined whenever they might return to this land. But Eli wanted more than to know the terrain, he wanted to know the people, and in a way that only men of Henry Craig's caliber would know them for he was a man that had sat in council with them, bartered in trade with them, lived with them, and had learned the language of many of the tribes, not just the common sign language, but the tongue of the different peoples. Eli learned that Craig had spent winters with both the Cheyenne and Arapaho, knew many of the people, and had come to know most of the prominent leaders.

"I was there many times when the chiefs came to trade with Dutch Bill, and sometimes when they tried talkin' to Hazen, but the general, he was kinda bull-headed, course he always laid it off on Sheridan and Sherman cuz they was his rankin' officers, but whenever any o' the chiefs wanted to talk peace or such like, Hazen'd say he didn't have the authority to make peace. 'Tween you'n me, he just wanted to take credit for the peace that was happenin' 'tween the Comanche and Kiowa Apache that was campin' out near Fort Cobb an' he knew if any others came, that might not stay peaceable," explained Henry.

Eli looked at the man and asked, "What about the raidin' parties that come north and hit the settlers and freighters? Sheridan seems to think they're all Cheyenne Dog Soldiers an' Arapaho renegades, cuz that's what we ran up against at the Arikaree."

Henry chuckled. "I was talkin' to Dutch Bill's Cheyenne wife, Jennie, one time, she's from Black Kettle's village, and she said there were quite a few young bucks that didn't like the peace talks, and they were the one's that were takin' off on raids to the northwest. She said it was cuz they were always gettin' shorted on their rations and ammunition for huntin' and such and the young bucks figgered they'd just take it from the settlers and such. She said whenever they came back, they'd share their bounty with the village and Black Kettle wouldn't say nothin to 'em."

"That seems to be the way it always is between generations, the youngsters feelin' their oats and thinkin' they know better, usually gettin' into trouble, causin' problems for the rest of the family. If I remember right, there mighta been a time or two that my elders thought that about me!" chuckled Eli, shaking his head as they continued their ride through the dry land country that was thick with tall dusty blue sagebrush, thick greasewood, and patches of bunch grass.

It was late on the second day after their skirmish with the natives by the Arkansas River that they crossed the Cimarron River just below the confluence with Bluff Creek. The banks of the river were thick with willow, indigo, dogwood and buttonbrush, while back from the water the thickets of cottonwood, elm and box elder stood almost unyielding to passersby, yet the scouts found the remains of an old trail that made the crossing easy in the shallows and cut through the heavy thickets. They made camp near the edge of the tree line, using a stand of elm for cover where the horses had graze and a trail to the water.

"How much further to the Washita?" asked Eli, stripping the gear from Rusty and Grey. The other men were doing the same with their animals and all were tired. It had been a long two days since their stand at the Arkansas, but they still had a ways to go.

"We'll cross the Canadian 'fore we get there, an' it'll be the afternoon of the second day."

"Think we'll have enough daylight to make a good scout, see who all's there?" asked Charlie.

"I think so, but what we don't see 'fore dark, we can see after first light. There are some tall red buttes that make for good lookouts. We can mount one o' them, see quite a ways up and downstream. 'Course, can't see it all from there, but quite a bit," responded Henry.

And it was mid-afternoon the next day when the three men came from a deep tree-shadowed gulley to climb the slopes of the red dirt butte that sat north of the Washita River. There were scattered scrub juniper, piñon, and some pin oak on the face of the butte, but the top was bald, save for some switchgrass and bluestem and scattered juniper. They tethered the horses at the juniper cluster, made their way to the southern edge of the butte and took cover behind some scrub juniper and settled in for a good survey of the valley of the Washita River below.

Henry had been here before and began pointing out the usual locations for the encampments of the different native peoples. "That ox-bow bend in the river, the point nearest us, is where Black Kettle has his camp of Cheyenne, looks to be about seventy, eighty lodges, but a couple them lodges look to be Arapaho, and maybe Lakota. That'd mean there's about three fifty, maybe four hundred people there."

"Who else is usually with Black Kettle?" asked Eli, who sat with his elbows on his knees, looking at the village on the south side of the river with his binoculars.

"Wal, Little Rock is his second chief, but there's also Big Man, Bear Tongue, Scabby Man, Wolf Looking Back, an' others. Dunno 'em all. His camp looks to be a good distance from the next 'un. We'll need to go downstream to get a look at the others."

They took to another red dirt butte further east and a little south of the other, but this was closer to the river and afforded a better view. Once again, they picketed their horses, took an observation point, and began scanning the terrain. The Washita River meandered with wide loops that resembled an oxbow, and Henry pointed out another village. "I'd say that's Little Raven's Arapaho, that lodge yonder, a little bigger'n the others, that's his lodge. That's the way the Arapaho are, a little more than the others. The chief's lodge is at the edge of the central grounds, faces east like the rest of 'em, but the chief's is always a little bigger, room for the council of elders. And you can see by the way it's laid out, that village has nigh unto two hundred lodges, but ain't none of 'em too far from the central dance grounds." Henry sat quiet a moment, looking at the land beyond the villages and more.

"You know any of the other leaders in that village?" asked Eli.

"Uh, lemme see, there's Spotted Wolf, Yellow Bear an' another'n I can't remember now."

Charlie pointed to the dip of the loop beyond the Arapaho village. "That looks to be Cheyenne, who would that be?"

Henry chuckled. "That's Medicine Arrows, he fancies himself a little more important than Black Kettle, but most of the folks don't think so, but that other village to the east there, that'd be Little Robe, he's considered number two under Black Kettle and if anything happens to Black Kettle, he'd be the one that'd take over. He also has Old Little Wolf, Stone Calf and Sand Hill. And that little village yonder, that's probably Old Whirlwind. What'dya figger is in the bunch?"

Eli had been looking at the many lodges while Henry explained and mumbled some numbers, "Near as I can figger, there's over a hundred, maybe a hundred an' fifty."

"So, how many people?" asked Charlie.

Henry grinned and shook his head. "If you was countin' all these an' them Comanche and Kiowa down by Cobb, I reckon you'd have, oh, maybe six, seven thousand people, prob'ly more."

Eli lowered his field glasses, looked at Henry as he whistled, "Oooeee, that's a bunch!"

"But without the Comanche and those further downstream?" asked Charlie.

"You mean what we looked at today?"

"Ummhmm."

"Maybe three thousand, maybe more. And of that they could field up to a thousand warriors," declared a somber Henry.

Eli looked at Charlie, glanced to Henry. "So, Henry, you headin' back to Cobb from here?"

"That's right, and I'm swingin' a little bit further north just to stay outta trouble." He nodded.

Eli looked to Charlie. "I think you an' me oughta be headin' due north and report back to Sheridan before he gets somebody in a heap of trouble."

"Then let's go. I'd like to find a good safe camp and have a good supper so I can sleep on a full stomach. We both might wake up dead if we hang around here too long!"

CHAPTER 20

REPORT

It was the end of October when Eli and Charlie rode back onto the grounds of Fort Hays. It had been a long, dry, cold return trip, but the men kept remembering the numbers of natives in their winter camp and wondering just what General Sheridan was planning, and both men knew it wouldn't be good. Charlie volunteered to take care of the horses while Eli reported to the general, although Eli was less than anxious to meet with him.

"Well, it's about time! Where you been galivantin' around to that took you so long?" declared Little Phil Sheridan with a mischievous grin splitting his face as he leaned back in his chair. He waved Eli to a chair and swung around to face him and asked, "So, find any?"

Eli nodded, his stoic expression saying more than he had words for at the moment. He sat down, removed his hat and ran his fingers through his hair and began, "General, I saw more Indians in one place on one day than I've seen all across the west in the rest of my life!"

The general leaned on his desk, scowling. "Explain."

But before he could begin, a knock at the door took his attention, and the general called out, "Enter!"

The door pushed open, and Colonel Custer walked in, gave a casual salute, and asked, "You wanted to see me, General?"

Eli remained seated, looked sidelong at Custer, and waited for Sheridan to speak.

"Yes, George." He paused, motioned to Eli, who stood and said, "This is Elijah McCain, he and his fellow scout just returned from an extended look-see to the south. He was about to give his report and I wanted you to hear it as well. Be seated."

Custer shook hands with Eli, nodding as he did and Eli did the same, until Custer said, "You were in the cavalry, weren't you?"

"I was, served with the general here, ended at Appomattox."

Custer nodded and sat down.

Eli looked to the wall to the right of the general where a big map hung and he stood, walked to the map and looked it over, found the locations he searched for and began. "Like you said, we went south, didn't see a lot of sign but there was some, so Charlie and me, we split up. I went east, Charlie west. That's where I met up with Henry Craig, a scout out of Fort Cobb." He looked back at the general who was nodding, and then continued. "He filled us in on what was happening at Cobb, and we decided to ride together. Went further south, ran into company A of the Tenth. They had been to Fort Dodge, and they helped to run off a band of Cheyenne and Kiowa, killed three, sent the rest on their way, and they were returning to Larned. They told us about a scrape they got into on Pawnee River with some Cheyenne."

He paused, looking at the map with a glance to the general. "Then we went south to the Arkansas, got jumped by a band of about a dozen young bucks, Cheyenne and Arapaho, killed six. And since Craig had the same orders as we did, to find the rest of the villages and get a head count, we found out he knew the tribes, wintered with some, and could tell us a little more than just how many."

"So, we went to the Washita, Black Kettle's camp, Little Raven's Arapaho, and more…"

He continued with his report and when he came to the final tally of more than six thousand natives and at least a thousand warriors, Eli paused. "So, we decided to come back and give you that report." He sat down, watched the general as he leaned back, looked at the map, glanced to Custer, thought a while, looked at some papers on his desk and lifted his eyes to Eli and Custer.

"You haven't told me anything I haven't suspected but did not know for sure. But what you've said just makes my task that much clearer. I've already started things moving." He paused, looked at the papers again and lifted tired eyes to Eli, shook his head slowly. "You remember Winchester, the Shenandoah valley, and more? That was done under direct orders from Grant, and he believed then, what he believes now, the only way to end the war then and to end this Indian war now, is to do the same thing. Destroy everything—when the people can't feed themselves, can't house themselves, then they will quit fighting!" He slammed his fist on the desk. "I hated it then and I hate it now! But Sherman believes it, and consarn it, I believe it! We've got to stop this continual fighting and killing!"

He paused, looked at Eli and Custer, and continued. "Now, Sherman sent dispatches to the commandants at

Dodge, Larned, Zarah, and Cobb. He wanted them to identify any native bands that are peaceful and willing to go to and stay on their reservation and not make any trouble. He's heard back from some, but not all. Colonel Hazen, down at Cobb, was expecting a visit from Black Kettle and Big Mouth of the Arapaho, but he was not optimistic. Sherman told Hazen to provide for any natives that were 'non-belligerent' and warned him I might have to pursue any hostiles and we want to be sure to spare the peaceable ones." He paused and looked at Eli. "But because of the raids that came from the Cheyenne and the Arapaho, Hazen already knows that I think those are hostile, no matter what they say."

The general stood and started pacing back and forth behind his chair, with glances to Eli and Custer as he began to explain. "Now, this is what I've done so far—I sent Armes and the Tenth with Hickok down to the Arkansas. They'll be following that upstream to Fort Lyon in Colorado and they're to engage the enemy at every opportunity! I sent Cody down to Larned, he'll be scouting from Dodge to Larned to Zarah and up to here, keeping the different troops abreast of any movements." He paused and sat back down. "Ultimately, there will be three columns converge on the hostiles' winter grounds, and if they're smart, when they see the numbers of troops, they'll lay down their arms and go to the reservations peacefully. One column will come from Fort Lyon, one from Fort Bascom in New Mexico, and of course our own Seventh that will be joined by the Nineteenth Kansas Volunteer Cavalry after they establish camp supply." Again, he paused, looking to the men for any reaction, but continued. "Now here's where you come in. You and Charlie and a couple others will go with Custer and the Seventh"—nodding to the colonel—"he's going to establish a camp, we'll call it Camp Supply, south of the Kansas border in Indian Territory. That will become my headquarters for the winter campaign against the natives. The colonel will lead his Seventh south, maybe to Washita to begin with, and depending on the response from the Cheyenne, like Black Kettle, and the Arapaho with Little Raven, will determine the rest of the campaign."

Eli sighed heavily, his shoulders lifting as he looked at the floor, up at the map and then to the general. "I ain't gonna like this." He spoke softly, shook his head, and asked, "When do we leave?"

"You've got a couple days to rest up, and resupply, and then the first week of November, you leave."

Eli nodded, stood, extended his hand to shake with Sheridan, then to Custer, and with a casual salute to the two, he turned away and left the office. He walked to the stables, his mind racing with all that was happening and might happen, and he asked himself, *Why did I get back into this?* He kicked at some rocks on the path, shaking his head as he walked and was relieved when he stepped into the shadows of the stable, saw Charlie sitting near the stalls and walked over to his friend.

Charlie looked up. "I can tell by your face the news ain't good!"

"We got a couple days to clean up, rest up, resupply, and then we leave."

"Where we goin' this time?"

"Back where we came from. We'll be scoutin' for Custer and the Seventh. They're goin' south to establish Camp Supply and that will be the headquarters for Sheridan and his winter campaign against the 'hostile' natives!"

Charlie dropped his eyes. "Glad I ain't hostile, no more, but…"

Eli dropped to the ground and seated himself near Charlie, both men leaning against the stall fencing, and asked, "But?"

"But I'm considerin' it."

"Considering what?"

"Much more of this, and I'll be gettin' a little hostile my own self!" grumbled Charlie.

"Me too," mumbled Eli.

———

IT WAS the end of the second day when Eli walked out of the stables, went to the westernmost edge of Fort Hays grounds and sat, legs outstretched, leaning back on his extended arms and lifted his eyes to the sky. The sun had tucked itself away, dragged all the colors of its pallet with it, and left behind the dark blue that was fading into black showing the distant horizon as a black line of shadow. The thin crescent of the moon hung low over the southwest sky, two stars were already lighting their lanterns, and Eli began a heart-to-heart talk with his Lord.

It was full dark when he rose, stretched, and started back across the darkened grounds to the stable. He and Charlie would sleep in the stable, get an extra early start in the morning, and leave before Custer and his men were ready. That would become the pattern of the two for the next couple weeks. Eli just was not real comfortable around Custer, preferring solitary time.

CHAPTER 21

SUPPLY

They rode on a golden carpet. With the late fall, the hardwood trees had held onto their leaves until the continuous cool forced them to lose their grip and the leaves of many hues drifted to the ground to form a deep carpet of golden shades for the travelers. Eli and Charlie rode south, staying in or near the trees for cover, crossed the Smoky Hill River and Walnut Creek, both showing signs of ice along the water's edge, and made camp on the south bank of Walnut Creek, to await the following Seventh Cavalry. Although the Seventh was to rendezvous with the nineteenth, the weather had kept the nineteenth from joining them before they left Camp Supply.

Dusk had dropped its curtain and the western sky had lost its color when the troops waded the creek and climbed down to make their camp. Each man was on his own, having carried his own rations, but several joined together to make cookfires and improvise the cold rations into a hot meal and coffee with it, and the fires sprinkled the south bank, marking the tree line of skeletal cottonwoods that stretched naked limbs to claw at the night sky.

Custer summoned the scouts to his fire and Eli and Charlie reluctantly left the warmth of their camp to make their way to the Colonel's camp. The man, keeping his image he so carefully cultivated while back in Washington campaigning for Andrew Johnson, sat with a buckskin coat, fringed at the sleeves and beaded across the chest, a campaign hat jauntily cocked to the side over his long locks of curly dusty blonde hair, and a stoic expression that was made more so by the drooping handlebar mustache and touch of whiskers under his lower lip. He frowned as Eli and Charlie came into the light of the fire and motioned the men to be seated on a grey log on the opposite side of the fire.

Custer looked at Eli and frowned. "You were at Appomattox, weren't you?'

"I was," answered Eli, without elaborating on his duties and rank while there.

"Thought so, you looked familiar when I met you in Sheridan's office." He dropped his eyes, looked about, and back to Eli and asked, "So, see anything of interest today?"

"No, nothing that would indicate natives on the move, if that's what you mean."

"Exactly. Now, the route we'll be going—south to the Arkansas, follow it till it bends west, then south to the Cimarron," explained Custer, glancing to the scouts.

Charlie dropped his eyes and cleared his throat. "It's a long way from the Arkansas to the Cimarron. You were thinking the confluence of Wolf Creek and Beaver River, well south of the Cimarron for the site of your camp, weren't you?"

Custer frowned, nodded, and waited for Charlie to explain.

Charlie continued. "When we leave the Arkansas, head due south, we'll cross Rattlesnake Creek, then we could hit one of the south moving creeks, there's three or four of 'em, down to Bluff Creek, cross it and follow Day Creek to the Cimarron."

Custer interrupted, "Right, right, then we follow the Cimarron south."

"Only if you want to add a couple days to your trip," mumbled Charlie, prompting Custer to frown and ask, "If not the Cimarron, what?"

"The Cimarron flows east thereabouts; we want to go south. It's mostly dry land but about fifteen miles south, we'll cross Buffalo Creek, then Sand Creek, then we'll be where you want to be at the confluence of Wolf and Beaver."

"Well, I reckon that's why Sheridan had you two as my scouts!" he chuckled. "How far you think, timewise, that'll be?"

"Another four, maybe five days," answered Eli, glancing to Charlie with a bit of a grin.

Charlie nodded, reached for the coffeepot and poured himself and Eli a cup. Charlie sipped the hot brew, lifted his eyes to the night sky to see the sliver of a moon snag the corner of a dark cloud, one of many across the sky that were hiding the night lanterns, and with a nod to Eli, he added, "But if we get snow, like I think we might, it'll take a while longer."

Custer frowned. "We're not slowing down for the weather, I don't care what it is!" he growled, reaching for his own cup.

———

BUT WHEN MORNING came and the men had to throw off blankets covered with snow, the grumbling and complaining of the men did little for the mood of the officers and even Custer with all his bluster, was slow getting around. By the time the troop was ready to leave, the scouts had been gone for over an hour and the trail they left was almost covered by the time the troop stretched out to follow. But Custer, always in the lead whether for travel or battle, led the men through the blowing snow as they hunkered down in their campaign coats and neck scarves, with their hats pulled low to keep the snow from their eyes. They made a short stop for nooning and to allow the men to brush the coats of the horses, try to dry them off with the few dry blankets that were passed around but soon useless, then kept moving until arriving at the Arkansas River just before dusk. The miserable, cold, and cantankerous men and mounts, struggled to make a camp and to get cover for both animals and man, but soon the cook fires winked at the darkness and the men were made comfortable. With full bellies and warm blankets, they slept some of the misery and murmuring away and awakened to a bright morning with a blazing sun that tempted them with a touch of warmth as they took to the trail to follow the river south.

By noon, the sun had melted the snow, leaving behind a muddy trail, but the constant wind of the prairies came from the northeast and made the men hunker down once again. And so it went for the next three days, blustery snow squalls, whistling cold winds, and cold camps, wet blankets, and more, all adding to the raft of complaints and criticisms of the troopers.

———

Eli and Charlie made their camp on the south bank of the Beaver River, the same river some were calling the North Canadian. They usually made their camp apart from that of the troopers and the Seventh was expected later that day or midday on the next. They had bagged a couple young whitetail bucks and had the loin of one sizzling over the cookfire as they waited for the coffee to perk and they sat near enough to the fire to enjoy the warmth, although little snow had fallen in this area, it was still a cool fall day. The rest of the fresh meat hung from a tall branch nearby, awaiting the arrival of the troops. Charlie was in a contemplative mood until he looked at Eli.

"I know why I don't like him, but how's come you don't like the famous Colonel Custer?"

Eli shook his head, his eyes glazing as he looked at the sizzling meat. "A man is not always what others think he is, or what they think about him, he's more than that. And it takes a while to really get to know a man, and I've always tried to reserve my judgment of a man until I get to know him and or know more about him. But Custer…" He shook his head as he thought back over the years. "I began hearing about him while in the war, and everything that came down about him just did not sit well. At West Point, he set a record, receiving more demerits than any other cadet ever. He graduated thirty-fourth out of 34, and most say that was only because they needed officers for the war. He came off as a man that was always looking for glory and was willing to do whatever, whenever to get recognition, and if he didn't, he would usually tell everybody how great he was. Oh, he was in a lot of battles, rose to leadership mighty fast, was known to lead the charge and be out front, and

I always heard good and bad about him. But when a man leads the charge for the glory of it like he did at Gettysburg, and loses 257 men, the only record that counts with me is that was the highest loss of any Union Cavalry, but he would later brag that charge was the most brilliant charge of cavalry ever made." He shook his head, remembering. "And when he was with Sheridan at Shenandoah, he did not hesitate to do his best to burn the entire valley off the map with no regard for the farmers, homeowners, workers, nothing!" He paused, poured some coffee, sat back, reflecting, "But it's the personal things also, after the war, he confiscated a very expensive prize racehorse named 'Don Juan' and when the owner wrote to General Grant and asked for his horse back, the general ordered Custer to return it, but he did not. He hid the horse, continued to race it and won prize money, until the horse died." He shook his head. "The rightful owner never did get any satisfaction out of that, and that tells me a lot about the character of the man."

Eli stood, stretched, reached for the coffeepot and poured another cup for himself and refilled Charlie's. He chuckled to himself, remembering, and looked at Charlie. "There was a book I read by the Roman poet, Ovid, who tells about a man named Narcissus, handsome fella that spurned all his potential lovers, and the gods punish him by making him fall in love with his own reflection in a pool. But when he found out that image could not love him back, he pined away and died." Eli chuckled. "Kinda like somebody else…"

They finished their meal, sat back with full bellies, and heard the approach of the troop. The tired bunch of troopers crossed the confluence, came near the camp of the scouts who motioned to the hanging meat, and the

Colonel turned to the men and ordered them to, "Start making camp! Pitch your tents, make your beds, start the cookfires. We'll have better eatin' tonight! The scouts have some fresh meat for you!"

CHAPTER 22

COBB

"So help me, sometimes I think this army and government is made up of idiots and fools!" declared a frustrated Brevet Major General William Hazen, commandant of Fort Cobb. He slammed his fist down on the desk, making the scattered papers jump, and stood and stomped to the window, mumbling to himself. He turned on his aide, Captain Henry Alvord who had been taking notes of the meeting with the Cheyenne chiefs Black Kettle and Little Robe and the Arapaho chiefs Big Mouth and Spotted Wolf. They had come seeking peace and declared themselves committed to having peace. They had asked to move their encampment to the protection of Fort Cobb, but Hazen had been forced to refuse.

Hazen stomped back to his desk. "Those were some of the greatest leaders of the natives of our time, and they have repeatedly tried for peace, signed treaties, did what they were asked, and some bumpkin that has never been out of his daddy's yard, nor away from his mother's apron strings, got him a job as an agent to the Indians, and he had never seen a real live native in his life, and he proceeds to ignore the treaty, demand the natives succumb to his wishes, and does everything he can to get everybody but himself killed just because he's too lazy to get out of his comfy cubby hole and wants them to come to him!" He slammed his fist on the desk again, fuming and mumbling.

"Have you ever heard of anything so stupid? It had to come out of Washington to be so stupid! They make a treaty that says the Cheyenne and Arapaho are to stay south of the Arkansas River, then demand they cross the river, go north to Fort Larned to get their annuities! So if they go north to get them, they break the treaty, if they break the treaty, they get no annuities!"

He jumped to his feet again, stomped to the window to watch the delegation of the two tribes leave the fort, shook his head, and looked at Alvord "Only a politician could be so stupid! I'd like to empty Washington, line 'em all up on the riverbank, and let the natives have target practice! Serve 'em right for bein' so arrogant!" He looked at his aide. "What else could I say when they wanted to move their villages down here—we already have Satanta, Lone Wolf, Black Eagle and their Kiowa Villages, and more Comanche and Kiowa Apache down-river." He mumbled again, "And Sheridan had already declared the Cheyenne and Arapaho as "hostile" because of their young bucks that are raiding north of the Arkansas, and unless I miss my guess, Sheridan is already making moves to attack them."

He plopped in his chair again, looked at his aide. "What else could I do? What would you do?"

Captain Alvord of the Tenth Cavalry set the paper and quill down on the corner of Hazen's desk, shook his head. "I don't know what else you could have done,

General. You told them it's not up to you but 'the great war chief, Sheridan'. But you will have to send a report to General Sherman."

"I know, I'll let you write it out, and tell him that if I had made peace with them, it would have brought them to Fort Cobb and Sheridan would probably follow them and we'd have another massacre like Sand Creek." He stood at his window, looked at the sky and saw the storm clouds moving closer and in the distance could see the wispy veil hanging below the clouds that told of a snow storm that was blanketing the plains, covering the land that Black Kettle and Big Mouth and their people would have to travel through. But they had a band of at least a hundred warriors, no women, and they were conditioned to the winter weather and would return to their encampment on the upper waters of the Washita River.

The storm had skirted the fort and Hazen was walking through the grounds and near the encampment of the Kiowa and Comanche and an elderly warrior stepped near and began to speak. "While you had council with the chiefs of the Cheyenne, our young warriors talked with their warriors and when they learned that you could not make peace, the warriors were pleased. They told our men that the Lakota and others would come down in the time of green-up and would drive out all the white men and blue coats. You should tell your people if they want to live, they must leave." The old man grinned a toothless grin, nodded, and walked away.

When Hazen returned to his office, he looked at his aide. "You sent off that report to Sherman yet?"

"Not yet, sir. It is almost ready though."

"Good," began the general as he began to explain about the young warriors and the threat of the Lakota and others coming south to drive out all white men.

"Add that to your report and request two more companies of the Tenth Cavalry from Arbuckle and throw in a couple howitzers while they're at it!"

———

WHEN BLACK KETTLE and the others left their encampment on the Washita to go to Fort Cobb, many young warriors of Black Kettle's camp joined together with young warriors of the camps of Old Whirlwind, Medicine Arrows and others, and the entire party of more than a hundred warriors went together with a band of Dog Soldiers and rode north on a raid of the white settlements in the Smoky Hill country. They returned from their raid the day before Black Kettle returned from Fort Cobb. But the raiding party had been spotted and trailed by Major Joel Elliott of the Seventh Cavalry who reported to Colonel Custer. This set in motion the plan of Custer to attack the encampments of the natives on the Washita River.

"We leave at first light!" was the last command given by Custer to the assembled junior officers of the Seventh Cavalry. The officers disbursed to their camps and began to spread the word to the troopers that they would start south with the coming of day. The orders were met with the usual grumbles and gripes, but the men turned in, hoping to get some sleep before the coming fight. The general gripe was as much against the weather, the continual flurry of snowstorms, as it was against the orders themselves. Yet many were anxious for the fight they had been told about and were looking forward to, for there is nothing as disheartening to a trained fighting man than to sit around, doing camp duties, instead of fighting.

———

BLACK KETTLE and the rest of the peace council returned from Fort Cobb to their encampment on the Washita just as a raiding party of Kiowa was returning from a raid of the Utes in Colorado territory and rode through Black Kettle's camp, headed for their own village further downstream on the Washita. One of their leaders, Lone Wolf, the younger, saw Black Kettle, and went to greet him. "Ho, Black Kettle, great chief of the Cheyenne, I am Namay-day-te, son of my father, Lone Wolf. We come from the land of the Ute, when we crossed the Canadian River, we saw a large trail of travelers, we believe them to be soldiers, leading southward toward the Washita camps. The trail was less than two hands old."

Black Kettle frowned. "Would not be blue coats, they do not come into this land in such weather! They like their warm lodges and would not leave them."

"That is for you to know, we go to our own village, further downstream. But there is one of our own, Trails the Enemy, he will stay a while with your people. There is a young woman, the sister of a friend, he is interested in seeing," chuckled Lone Wolf, grinning to the chief as both men understood the way of the young warriors.

Black Kettle was not a man to make hurried decisions and was respected as a leader because he often called together the council to discuss such concerns. One of the warriors known as Bad Man, approached him. "Black Kettle, I spoke with Crow Neck, he was one that went on the raid with the Dog Soldiers. He said he had to leave his tired horse on the trail and went back to get him earlier this day. He said he saw many on the far trail that he thought were soldiers. He was afraid, returned without his horse to tell me, but I think he was just feeling bad because he went on the raid with the others.".

Black Kettle answered, "You are probably right, Crow Neck is not a brave man." Bad Man nodded, turned away to go to his lodge. Black Kettle looked to the lowering sun, summoned a nearby warrior and sent him to gather the leaders of the village to a council. He glanced to the sky and the gathering storm clouds, shook his head and gathered his buffalo robe around his shoulders and went to his lodge to await the leaders.

As the council gathered, Black Kettle told of what they had learned at Fort Cobb about the great war leader of the bluecoats, Sheridan, and his war plans. The council talked for several hours, some hopeful, many skeptical, but finally decided in the early morning hours to follow the suggestion of Little Robe. "I say we send runners to see if these are soldiers, and if so, tell them we wish to talk peace."

"It is good!" declared several of the others, most nodding their heads in agreement, some because they were tired and wanted to return to their own lodges, but White Shield, Black Hawk's brother, spoke before they finished, "We should move our camp. If the soldiers are coming and will not talk peace, we should find a better place if we must fight. We should move tonight! I have had a vision of our band scattered and destroyed."

"We could go to the camp of Whirlwind. We would be stronger and in a better place," offered Black Hawk.

Little Robe and others nodded their heads in agreement, mumbled expressions of accord, looked to Black Kettle, but the chief said, "There is much snow, the soldiers will not move in such, and we will wait to hear from the runners. Then we will move."

When the leaders left the lodge, Black Kettle's wife, Medicine Woman, entered, anger flaring in her eyes as she confronted her husband. "We must leave tonight! We could have moved before, I do not like this delay. There are too many signs. Are we crazy and deaf that we cannot hear the spirits?" she growled as she moved about the lodge, rearranging things in her frustration, but Black Kettle remained seated, legs crossed, watching his woman and shaking his head.

CHAPTER 23

SEVENTH

Contrary to what they had done before, Eli and Charlie rode near the front of the column with the senior officers, Custer, Captains Myers, Thompson, Benteen and Major Elliot. Custer looked to Eli. "I want you two to lead us south to the Washita, but as we near the area, my Osage scouts will move in first and get closer and will be scouts for each of the battalions to scout where I'll be sending our units."

"That's fine, Colonel, whatever you want."

Eli had been aware of the band of Osage scouts favored by Custer and knew how he used the dozen men who were lifelong enemies of most of the plains Indian tribes. Although Custer had not been a good student at West Point, he had become enamored with the use of guerrillas in close-in fighting. It was a style of warfare used in the Peninsular war between Spain and France and had been very effective. Custer had used his Osage scouts in much the same surreptitious manner very effectively. The Osage rode in a unit behind the First Battalion of cavalry and usually kept to themselves.

Following the Osage, the musicians of the Seventh rode, followed by the remaining battalions. Custer had dismissed the leaders of the battalions, and they rode back to take the lead of each of their commands.

It was late afternoon of the third day out of Camp Supply and the terrain, although under the snowfall of the last three days, the wind had drifted the snow and piled it in the draws, ravines, and around any cluster of trees and brush, giving the land a red and white patch-work quilt look. The red soil of the land contrasted with the bright white of the snowdrifts, but the troopers paid little attention to the scenery, with chins tucked into collars, hats pulled down and wrapped with scarves to keep them on and cover their ears, the men improvised anything at hand to dispel the miserable cold. After crossing the Canadian, Custer called a halt for their last meal before Washita. He allowed the men to make cook-fires as the supply wagons had fallen well behind and the men would have to make do with whatever rations they carried.

Custer had summoned all the scouts, Eli, Charlie, and the Osage to his fire and turned to Eli. "Would you draw us a diagram on how you remember the camp of the Cheyenne on the Washita?" He motioned to an area of red soil where the snow had been scraped away and Eli grabbed a stick and began to draw a diagram with the meandering course of the Washita as the central part. He looked to Charlie often for any input but began to draw and talk. "The river makes a big bend, like an 'S'. Here at the bottom is the camp of Black Kettle, but the river turns back north, makes another big loop, and there are camps here"—making an 'X' near the top of the bend, and another just around the bend—"and here. Henry Craig said this one up top is Little Raven's Arapaho, and this'n"—pointing to the one past the bend—"is Satanta, the Kiowa chief. And on around that bend and where the river turns back east, is another Cheyenne camp, probably Old Whirlwind."

"Good, good," declared Custer, as he stood and accepted the drawing stick from Eli and began to explain to his scouts and the officers that had joined them, his plan for their attack on the village. When all the questions had been asked and answered, Custer stood. "Now, see to your men, and have something to eat. We'll be moving out soon and will arrive to take up our positions well after dark. Caution your men to silence, secure any canteens, sabers, anything that will make noise, and good luck, men."

The terrain they crossed at any other time of the year would show sagebrush, cholla, piñon, and juniper. The red dirt contrasted with the bunch grass and the blue of the sage and grey of the greasewood, but now snow blanketed the land giving the appearance of a downy blanket that lay quietly across the rolling hills and offering a look at the land that is seldom seen, that of low rolling hills unmarred by rocky escarpments, deep scarred ravines, and twisted skeletons of long-dead trees. The four abreast column trudged ever southward, as the sun made its escape in the west behind the dark storm clouds but gave a silver lining to the clouds that held its own beauty.

The darkness was dissipated slightly by a half-moon that rose above the scattered clouds. The storms had subsided, and the wind calmed, as the long column of the Seventh came through the hills toward the Washita. As the river made a bend to the south, Custer stopped the column, used signals to summon the officers forward, and when they arrived, he pointed out the bend of the river, the shadowy buttes on the north side that would be used to shield their approach, and the long tree line that marked the banks of the Washita. He looked at the men.

"The bugler will sound the charge, that'll be about the first crack of dawn, but wait for the bugler to charge. Have your men assembled, quiet, and ready. Elliott will come from the east flank, Thompson from the south, Myers from the west, and I'll come across the river from the north. All clear?"

The officers nodded, mumbled an agreement and at the wave of Custer, the four men resumed their places with their battalions and began moving them into position. They would bide their time while in position, readying themselves as the grey light of early morning approached.

Eli nodded to Charlie and the two moved off to the side, taking to a thicket of juniper apart from the others. Eli reined up, stepped down, and Charlie did the same. They loosened the girths on their horses, found a comfortable place to stretch out and as they did Eli explained, "It was clear to me that Custer was wanting only his Osage doin' the scoutin' now, so, we'll just be spectators come mornin'."

"Suits me! I wasn't anxious to get scalped," declared Charlie, stretching out on his blankets. He crossed his ankles, put his clasped hands behind his head and looked through the branches of the big juniper to see the sparkle of a couple stars. He grinned and turned to look at Eli. "This ain't no time to be makin' war, ya' reckon?"

"Is there ever a good time?" responded Eli.

"What're you gonna do after this little shindig is over?"

"Dunno, but if there's gonna be more like this, I'm prob'ly gonna hightail it outta here."

———

A LONG LINE of low-rising knolls stood about sixty to eighty feet higher than the flats between the knolls and the tree line at river's edge, and it was behind this line of knolls that most of the Seventh took up their position prior to the attack. Both Eli and Charlie were restless and rose from their blankets, tightened the girths on their saddles and mounted up for a ride around to see what was going on with the troops. Their temporary camp was about twelve hundred yards back from the bend in the river that hid the village of the Cheyenne, the tree covered knolls offered good cover, but Custer did not allow any fires, knowing even the smallest fire could be seen for miles on a dark night, and the smell of woodsmoke was also easily detected.

When Eli and Charlie neared the camp of Custer, they saw the fringed buckskin coat of the Colonel's as he moved about, nervously pacing and slapping his leg with a quirt, thinking about the coming fight. He saw Eli and Charlie, and motion to the side showed the return of three of the Osage that had been sent on a scout of the village. Custer signaled them all near and listened as the Osage gave their report.

The first man, Tall Moon Rising, began. "The village is quiet, even the dogs are inside the lodges. The snow makes things quiet, and the horse herd is beyond the village. If there are watchers, they must be in the trees taking shelter, nothing moved near the horses."

Custer nodded, and asked, "How many lodges?"

"Too many to count. Ten times two hands, and again."

"Two hundred?"

"Maybe more, maybe less."

Eli spoke up. "What about the other divisions, from Fort Lyon and Fort Bascom?"

"Probably the same as the Nineteenth Volunteers, held up by the snow. But we're not waiting for them. The plan has not changed, we strike at dawn!" He looked to Eli and Charlie. "I want you two to check on the other battalions, Elliot should be there"—pointing to the east at the edge of the bluffs—"and Myers and Thompson should be near the river, there"—he pointed to the south of his own position. "Make sure they're ready and report back to me." He looked at the stars, back to Eli. "You think we have another hour or a little more before light?"

"Looks to be about right, Colonel."

Custer looked to the Osage. "You and the rest of your scouts, swing north of the big bend, check on the other villages. If there's any movement, send the report back to me of what's happening. The last thing we need is for the rest of the villages to spring a trap on us as we attack one village." He shook his head, turned away as if dismissing the others and walked toward the bivouacked troops.

Eli glanced to Charlie, and both men returned to their mounts and started for Elliot's position. Within the hour, they had checked with the other battalions, found them all ready and anxious, and reported back to Custer, just as the thin line of grey tore the night sky from the black horizon beyond the tree line at the river where the Washita bent back to the north and stood as a barrier between the troops and the sleeping village.

CHAPTER 24

GARRY OWEN

The village was quiet and still, the dark shadows of the lodges lay peacefully on the snow, the white blanket lay soft on the ground, adding a stillness to the sleeping village. Even the usual dogs were huddled inside the lodges or had crawled comfortably under the stacked hides and gear at the back of the lodges, tails tucked under their bellies, noses pushed between cold paws. The blanket at the opening of a lodge was tossed back, but no light showed, and a hunched figure stepped out, the heavy buffalo robe giving the impression of hunch backed, but the barrel of a rifle protruded between the folds and the slow-moving figure made his way to the trees, that age-old awakening that often troubled the sleeping drove him to the edge of the river. He struggled with the heavy robe, grumbling to himself, and stood spread-legged, and lifted his eyes to the shadows amid the blend of moonlight and the coming dawn. His eyes grew large, and he fumbled for his rifle, jacked a round into the chamber and lifted it to the sky, and Double Wolf screamed as he pulled the trigger, sending the blast of the discharge echoing through the hills and across the river. He grabbed at the fallen robe, turned, and started at a run to the village, shouting and screaming, stumbling and dragging the big heavy robe.

"Nótàxéve'ho'e!" he screamed, again and again, trying to awaken the village.

When the rifle shot sounded, the horses of the soldiers jerked as did the men at the unexpected blast, but the shot prompted Custer to give the signal to the bugler who lifted the cold bugle to his lips and sounded 'Charge'! No sooner had the last note of the bugle's command dropped from the cold air than the musicians that Custer had assembled near the trees, began to play *Garry Owen* to further signal the attack. Custer's battalion surged behind him as his horse lunged into the cold water of the Washita River, thin layers of ice crowded around the horses' legs and the big horse humped and lunged and lunged again, taking him to the far bank.

Custer stood tall in his stirrups, turned slightly to his men and screamed to his more than two hundred men, "Charge!!" His saber standing high above him as he signaled his men onward.

Simultaneous to the beginning of the charge by Custer's Battalion, Major Elliot's battalion numbering over a hundred fifty, surged to the east to make its sweep to swing around, cross the river, and come at the village from the east flank. Captains Myers and Thompson had stood ready on the north bank of the river and at the command, their battalions, each about a hundred fifty strong, surged forward and splashed across the river. Once across they turned to the east to strike at the village from the west and south flanks. Custer's battalion struck first and drove directly through the village, shooting, screaming, slashing with sabers, and striking at anything and anyone that moved or stood waiting. A woman with child in her arms and another holding tightly to her leggings, ran between the lodges, pursued by a trooper with stripes on his sleeves and lifting his Colt Dragoon revolver, aiming at the fleeing woman. The pistol bucked, roared, spouted lead and the woman stumbled, but the trooper neither reined up nor stopped his mount, driving the big bay horse over the woman and her child, stomping them into the ground. The trained cavalry horses of all the men drove through the melee, stomping on anything and anyone that fell before them.

The warriors grabbed rifles, pistols, bows, lances, war clubs, anything to try to defend their village and their families. Screams told of life slipping from bodies, both those clad in buckskin and those covered in blue, but most soon bore the same blood red as life became cheap and was quickly snatched from men, women, and children. The drone of battle, gunshots, screams, horses whinnying, children crying, the crackle of fire as lodges were set aflame, the thunder of hooves as the cavalry charged, and with each battalion's assault, the melee mounted and the stench of battle rose above the village and marred the air of the wilderness, as the pure blanket of white became stained with splashes of blood and scattered with broken bodies. Every charge through the village brought more and more blood and screams and each charge ended with the entire battalion turning and driving back through the village, each time a little different angle of assault, but the results were the same. Occasionally a trooper would slide from his mount and grab a fleeing woman or child, usually catching them by the hair and dragging them back to the waiting horse.

One trooper called, "Gotcha one, eh Smitty?"

"Ain't the first! We're takin' 'em yonder to the trees!" He cackled, grinning a lustful grin. "Better gitcha one while the gittin's good, Smoky!"

The assault lasted well over an hour and as it began to subside, more were seen chasing possible captives to gather them in a bunch at the tree line. Other troopers were torching the lodges and stacks of goods, even throwing some bodies into the flames. The smell of burning flesh mixed with the stench of loosed bowels, emptied stomachs that had been slashed open, burning hides and blankets and more as lodges with winter's supply of food, clothing, and more, lifted to the sky in ashes.

Eli and Charlie joined Custer who had ridden through the village leading his men in the initial charge, but once through he ordered his men to "Destroy everything you see!" He rode to the southeast to a knoll that rose above the flats and offered a view of the battle. The men stepped down from the horses and while Custer grinned, clenched his fists and mumbled encouragement to his men, Eli and Charlie winced, shook their heads and watched in revulsion at the acts of the men.

As the men in blue attacked and chased after fleeing natives, they had seen the lust of blood, fire of anger, rage of power, and drive of battle in the eyes of the men. Eyes that flared with the adrenaline that surged through their bodies, but the blood lust that drove them to slash and shoot again and again at any living being, man, woman, child, infant, dogs and more drove the men on. Riding through the village in a rage, the men would most often swing their mounts around, dig spurs into their ribs and charge back through the melee so often that both horse and men were covered with blood and detritus, with an appetite that never seemed to wane.

Women clasping infants in their arms fled from the village, seeking refuge in the trees at the river's edge or in the deep grasses in the flat. Time and again, Eli and Charlie saw soldiers that had seen the runaways would give chase and slash them down as they rode past, giving no heed to women or children. Occasionally a man in blue would try to give quarter, let someone live, but would often have to flee himself to avoid being gunned down or end up on the end of a lance. During the charge, Captain Benteen, who had ridden with Elliott, saw a young man lift a pistol and fire a shot in his direction, but the captain did not return fire until the young man lifted the pistol again and took aim, and in defense of himself, Benteen fired a kill shot that took the young man down, but he hung his head and shook it in disgust at himself, but also knew there was no other way.

From the crest of the knoll, the watchers saw Major Elliot strike the northeast point of the village, but when a band of warriors surged from the trees behind them, they turned to face the attack and gave chase. The watchers also saw warriors coming from other camps and they would find out later those warriors came from the Arapaho, Kiowa, and Cheyenne camps to assist Black Kettle's band.

Custer turned to Benteen who had led a squadron with Elliot, but when Elliot gave chase after the warriors from the other camps, Benteen finished their charge on the east flank, and retired to the hill with Custer. "Get the bugler, sound recall, and we'll face off against that new threat!" He pointed to the gathering warriors on the knolls to the east of the flats. As he spoke Charlie motioned to the far rise and saw many other warriors gathering there, watching the battle. Custer nodded.

"We'll go after them first!" he declared, swung aboard his mount, and followed Benteen toward the village.

As he approached the battle, Custer was approached by Tall Moon Rising, Walks Far, and War Shield, three of the Osage scouts. He ordered them, "Start driving the horses into the flats to the south, we'll keep about two hundred, kill the rest!"

Tall Moon's eyes flared, and he cocked his head to the side. "Kill them?"

"That's right. Shoot them. If the Cheyenne have no horses, they cannot go on raids. When we destroy their food, clothing, lodging, and horses, they will go to the reservation."

When Custer assembled his men, he did not go to the aid of Major Elliot, instead he knew he had to face the threat of the other villagers joining the fight and he gave the order to form a two-deep line across the flat, turn to face the threat, and start the charge at a walk. It was more of a bluster and bluff, because he remembered the report from Eli and Charlie that told of six thousand people and more than a thousand warriors. The fight they already were in was more than enough and he wanted to make the others believe they would charge them and do to their villages what had been done to Black Kettle's village.

The ruse worked and the watching warriors dropped off the bluffs and returned to their villages and Custer regrouped his men to return to the burning remains of Black Kettle's village. As he neared the remains, he looked at the scattered bodies, the destroyed lodges, the waste of war, but he sat tall in his saddle seeing this as a victory and the remains of the village the evidence of the vanquished. He barked commands, "You!" shouting to a group of three soldiers that were desecrating the bodies of two warriors. "Burn the rest of the lodges, destroy all their goods!"

As he rode through the remains of the village, he repeatedly issued similar orders. When he saw Captains Myers and Thompson, he barked, "Thompson! Gather your men, go to the herd of horses there"—motioning to the south flats—"destroy the horses!" He looked at the other man. "Myers! Gather the captives, herd them over near the trees. Get 'em ready, we'll bring some horses over for 'em. We'll be takin' 'em back to the camp."

Eli and Charlie had come from the knoll, rode around the edge of the village, heard Custer barking his orders, stopped, and looked around. Eli turned in his saddle to see the soldiers and Osage scouts start shooting the horses. It was something that a man of the wilderness just could not stomach. A man's horse becomes an extension of himself and ofttimes the only friend and ally he may have in hard times. Eli's quick estimate was six to seven hundred horses slaughtered and he could not help but remember the work his men had done to drive a herd of a thousand all the way from California for the cavalry to have remounts. He shook his head at the wanton destruction, felt sick to his stomach, looked at Charlie. "Let's go back to Camp Supply, I need to talk to Sheridan."

The two friends returned to their makeshift camp, gathered the rest of their gear and mounted up, but as they turned for one last look at the carnage and destruction, they saw Custer order the battalions about, and they frowned as they saw the officers ordering the men to put the captive women and children on horses, but as the columns started to the trail, all the captives were at the rear of the columns, literally shielding the troopers from any shooting or attack from the rear.

Eli looked at Charlie and the looks exchanged told of the friends' common disgust at the sights they had seen and the carnage and more they had witnessed. As they started north, they took their own trail, staying apart from the troops, and they traveled in silence, the cold air of early evening piercing their spirits and prompting them to hunker down in their coats, but while they were silent and the shuffling of hooves in the remaining snow gave little sound, their minds were awash with recriminations and accusations and judgments, both for themselves and the many others that were part of this day's historical massacre, and massacre was what it was, for they could call it by no other name.

CHAPTER 25

REPORT

With only a couple hours of daylight left, the columns made camp on the south bank of the Canadian River. With thickets of cotton-wood, black walnut, bur oak and more, there was ample cover and shelter from the howling winds of winter whose very moans in the night chilled the bones of the men. Eli and Charlie also camped on the south bank, but well away from the troopers, yet their fire was seen and before they finished their meal, they heard the approach of a single horse and when it came into the firelight, they were surprised to see Captain Benteen.

"Evenin' Captain. Step down, we've got coffee to spare," offered Eli, frowning and wondering just what this visit might be about.

The captain stepped down, ground tied his mount and moved to the grey log that faced the small cookfire. He sat down, held his hands out to the warmth of the flames that licked at the wood, and looked up to Eli. "I want to ask a favor."

"Go ahead, Captain. 'Course listenin' to the request

does not guarantee a suitable answer," chuckled Eli, glancing to Charlie and back to the captain.

"I believe you were on the knoll with Custer when they saw Elliot take a squadron and give chase to the natives that came from the other camps, is that right?"

"Yeah, we saw that, but they went into the trees, and we couldn't see what happened. Did he make it back?"

"No, and Custer did not go after them or send anybody to find them. We left with no word," grumbled Benteen, grabbing a stick and throwing it angrily at the fire causing embers to take flight into the night sky.

"And you want us to go back and find out what happened to them?"

"That's right. Major Elliot is a friend of mine and for Custer to just forget about him and the twenty or so men with him, just…well…" He shook his head, unable to find the words to describe his boiling emotions.

Eli glanced to Charlie, saw his minimal head nod, and looked back to Benteen. "We'll do it, Captain. We'll get us a little sleep and start out 'fore first light."

Benteen stood, obviously relieved. "Thanks McCain…" He paused, remembering, squinted a little and cocked his head to the side. "Are you the same McCain, Colonel McCain that was with Sheridan at Appomattox?"

Eli nodded, letting a slow grin split his face.

"Thought so. Didn't expect to see you as a scout, you were a well-respected cavalry officer, thought you'd stay in and rise through the ranks."

Eli grinned, slowly shaking his head, and did not answer the implied question.

———

THE MOON that hung lazily in the southwestern sky, was waxing toward full when the two rolled from their blankets. Much of the snow had been blown into the trees, gullies, and patches of dark showed across the flats that stretched to the south. The horses had been content in the shelter of the trees and now grudgingly stepped out to cross the grassy flats and move through the snow-crusted waves of grass, sage, and greasewood.

The Washita was about fifteen miles south and the thin line of grey-blue made silhouettes of the few flat-topped mesas that sat low on the land, giving the only break in the monotonous flat line of horizon. Directly south, they could see the shadowy line of the buttes that had sheltered the troops before the attack and further on the tree line of the Washita. Eli reined up, sat looking into the dark land, glanced to Charlie.

"I think Elliott's bunch went around the point of this line of buttes, crossed the river there, and after striking the village, took off after the warriors from the other camps to the east-northeast. That the way you remember it?" he asked, looking to Charlie, who sat hunched on his saddle.

The collar of his coat turned up, and his chin, which was wrapped with his scarf, tucked into the collars to avoid the rising cold wind. He nodded as his only answer and Eli nudged Rusty in that direction.

They rounded the point of the buttes, pushed toward the shadows of the tree line, and at a break that had been made by the passing of the troopers, they crossed the shallows of the Washita. Once across, they broke into the open and reined up to look about. Charlie stepped down, looked closely at the tracks made by the many riders, and after a few moments, he looked up to Eli. Pointing to the west and the remains of the village. "Here's where

Benteen and the others went to the village." He paused, turned and pointed to the scattered trees that were sprinkled across the grassy flat. "There's where Elliott chased the others." With a glance to Eli, Charlie mounted up and the two followed the tracks into the shadowy flat.

The eastern sky was showing red, the storm clouds blushed pink on the bottom, and the light gave guidance to the two scouts searching for Elliott. They rode through the scattered trees, and the flutter of wings as many turkey buzzards lifted, told the two men they had found the soldiers. Scattered about were the remains of more than twenty men, all had been stripped, mutilated, and desecrated by the carrion eaters, buzzards, coyotes, magpies, crow, bobcats, badgers, eagles and others. There was nothing recognizable about any of the men and it was only because Eli and Charlie knew these remains had to be what was left of the squadron led by Elliott. They walked among the remains, looking, shaking their heads, searching for anything that might identify anyone and it was only when Charlie saw something shiny at the foot of one body, he knelt to examine it and pulled out the saber that had been engraved with *Major Joel Elliott, Seventh Cavalry.*

Charlie handed the saber to Eli and both men walked back to their ground-tied mounts, swung aboard, and started back north to return to Camp Supply. Silence hung like a blanket about them, what they had seen would be something that could not be erased from their memories nor their consciousness. The stench of rotting flesh and the smell of death hung heavy over the scene and followed them as they left. It was only the morning breeze that offered any freshness to the air that lay on the land.

Eli and Charlie pushed their mounts and themselves and covered the normal three-day ride back to Camp Supply in two long days, arriving shortly after the entire Seventh Cavalry rode into the post. Eli and Charlie rode directly to the commandant's tent and were ushered into the tent to report to Sheridan. Custer was already seated before the general, and Sheridan nodded with a smile to Eli and motioned him and Charlie to take a seat on the edge of the cot. Sheridan looked at Eli. "Good to see you Eli, Charlie. Custer was just giving his report."

"And what was the report, General?" asked Eli, glancing from Custer to Sheridan.

Sheridan looked down at his notes, up to Eli. "He reported fifteen of his men were wounded, three dead. Of the Cheyenne, he said there were at least 105 dead, sixty captives, and no count of how many were wounded. All in all, that's a good report and I'm pleased." He nodded as he spoke, and grinned as he looked from Eli to Custer and back.

"You might want to amend that a little, General," began Eli with a glance to Custer, whom he asked, "That didn't include Elliott's command, did it?"

"Well, no. Major Elliot disobeyed my orders and gave chase to a few renegades and left Benteen in charge of the attack on the village. Elliott has not reported in."

Eli nodded, reached behind him and brought out the saber, handed it hilt first to the general who was frowning as he accepted it, looked at the engraving and lifted his eyes as he scowled at Custer. Eli explained, "Major Elliott gave chase when additional warriors from the other camps attempted to go to the aid of Black Kettle's band. He was caught in an ambush and his entire squadron of at least twenty men were slaughtered."

Sheridan's eyes flared, as he looked from Eli to Custer and stated, "Explain!"

Custer fidgeted about, looking from Sheridan to Eli and to the ground, then began. "It's like I said, Major Elliott disobeyed orders. He was to lead his battalion around to the east and attack the village from the east. We saw from the bluff to the south, that he turned away from the village and took off into the trees. Yes, there was a handful of warriors that came from those trees, but not enough of a threat to split his command."

"Why didn't you go to his aid?"

"There were others from the different villages that had appeared and looked to be ready to attack. I mustered my men, formed an attack line and feinted an attack to dispel them, and they turned tail and ran. I thought Elliott would return and we set about mopping up the fight, destroying the horse herd and the rest."

Eli stood, glanced from Custer to Sheridan. "General, we"—nodding to Charlie—"rode most of the night to get here and we're played out. If it's alright with you, we'd like to turn in and get some sleep. We'll come back first thing in the morning, if you need us."

Sheridan nodded, looked from Eli to Custer, and answered, "That'd be fine, Eli. We'll talk in the mornin'."

Eli and Charlie left, and judging by the tone of the general and the look that was given, Eli thought the general wanted some private time with the flamboyant Custer. Besides, he was feeling crowded in the small tent, what with the two of them, the general, Custer and his ego, it was considerably uncomfortable.

Chapter 26

Decision

H e had put it off as long as he could until he begrudgingly gave in to his responsibility and started to the camp where the battalions were bivouacked, and the officers' tents were arranged at the end of the long line of troopers' wall tents. Eli and Charlie had pitched their camp in a cluster of juniper away from the camp and now he walked back to meet with General Sheridan. When he suggested Charlie accompany him, Charlie frowned, shook his head.

"Great war chief don't want to talk to no Injun!" he grumbled and turned away to begin packing their gear.

When Eli approached the wall tent of the general, he noticed many of the men had already been put to work making the camp a little more permanent. Two of the supply wagons had been stripped of their canvas and were returning from the Beaver River with loads of logs. Other men were busy digging holes, readying the trench for the butts of the logs that would make up the stockade for the fort. It was evident that Sheridan's plans were going forward, and he was making preparations to continue his winter campaign against the natives.

As Eli approached, a corporal was standing guard at the entry and stopped Eli. "The general is busy, you'll have to wait."

"Any idea how long?" asked Eli.

But the general had heard his voice and called out, "If that's McCain, let him come in!"

Eli grinned. "That's me," he said, and walked past the corporal and pushed open the entry flap to enter the tent. Eli did not want a confrontation with Custer and was relieved to see the general was just busy with paperwork and was glad to see Eli to give him a break with the details. "Mornin' Eli, did you get some rest?" asked Sheridan.

"I did, thanks, General, and you?"

"Same, but duty prevails and there's much to do," he stated, waving a hand over the papers on his makeshift desk, and waved Eli to be seated.

Eli sat down, removed his hat and ran his fingers through his hair as he looked at the general. This man had been a friend for many years, and he hated to fail him in any way, but he and Charlie had made their decision, and he was determined to stand by it. He looked at the general and began, "General, we did not mean our report to get anyone in trouble, but I knew you would not get the entire picture without what we had to say. I know Custer was acting on your orders and you were acting on the orders from Sherman, but you said you agree with the plan and were committed to it. I understand that and don't fault you for it. I know you believe that is the only way to put a stop to this incessant raiding and killing." He dropped his eyes, shook his head, and continued. "But isn't that the same that peoples have been doing for centuries? When one people wants the territory or treasures of another, they go against them in war, overpower or destroy them, and seek to make the survivors into their own image—to believe the same, dress the same, live the same, worship the same gods, literally to become just like their conquerors as if their way is the only way or the best way?"

"General, these people, the natives, have had their own way of living, their own culture, for decades if not centuries, and we, the superior white race come in, take away their way of life and their very lives, seeking to remove them or at least to remove any semblance of their way of life, making them become like us or be destroyed. And we fault them for fighting to keep their lands, their homes, their families, their way of life." He slapped his leg with the hat he held and had crumpled up, frustration painted on his face. He let out a heavy sigh and shook his head. "So,

Charlie and I are headed north. We're going to the Oregon Trail, maybe hook up with a wagon train, maybe just wander the wilderness for a while. We need some fresh air and it's in short supply hereabouts."

The general sat silent and still, looking at Eli, obviously pondering what had been said, then dropped his eyes, slowly shook his head, and spoke softly. "I understand. I told you at the outset of this that I agreed with it, but I also hated it, and I do. But I had to make a choice, bury natives or bury settlers and after the war, I was tired of burying our own people. I know this does not make it right, this policy of complete desecration, but if it lingered on for many years, there would be even more, both white and red, that would also have to be buried. I believe this will hasten the end."

He looked directly at Eli, stood, and extended his hand. "I thank you for what you've done. The horses you supplied, the scouting you've done, and the friendship you've given. May we meet again under better circumstances."

The men shook hands and the little general pulled Eli close and wrapped his arms around his friend, then let him go and leaned back. "You've been a good friend and a loyal one. I'm thankful." Eli turned to leave, glanced back to the general and exited the big wall tent. The sun shone bright, the day was clear, and he did his best to straighten his crumpled hat and put it on his head, as he started back to the camp and the waiting Charlie.

"How'd it go?" asked a grinning Charlie. He sat by the little cookfire where the coffeepot was showing steam rising and Charlie was holding a cup of the steaming brew with both hands as he sat with elbows on his knees, looking expectantly to his friend.

Eli grinned. "Good, you ready?"

"Gotta finish muh java, you want some?"

"Of course," stated Eli as he sat down opposite his friend.

Charlie poured him a cup and handed it across to Eli, then asked, "So, I know we're leavin', headin' north, but then what?"

Eli chuckled, shrugged, and answered, "Dunno, we'll just wait'n see, I reckon. But I did have a thought about maybe joinin' up with a wagon train, if we come across one, but if not, we'll just head to the mountains and enjoy ourselves."

"Uh, you do know it's winter in them mountains?"

"Well, yeah," answered a grinning Eli.

"And any wagon trains headin' into the mountains would be full o' people whut ain't got no sense?"

"Prob'ly, but we've met up with quite a few folks that fit that description."

"Don't mean I wanna hang out aroun' 'em. Ain't that what we been doin'?" He waved his hand toward the many wall tents that made up Camp Supply.

"Ah, that's just the officers, lot o' those fellas are good men."

"Which ones? The last I noticed all of 'em were ridin' through Black Kettle's village with blood on 'em," grumbled Charlie.

Eli shrugged, tossed the dregs of his coffee and put the cup and the pot in the pannier aboard the grey and went to Rusty, gathered the reins in hand, stuffed his foot in the stirrup and swung aboard the big stallion. Rusty pranced a little to the side, bent his head around to look at his rider, tossed his head, and stepped out, anxious to be on the trail. It was as if the big claybank knew they were leaving the confines of the Army and were headed to fresh air and freedom, and he was anxious for both.

It was unusual, but for two weeks, the travelers had fair weather, with nothing more that cold nights and cool winds and midday on the fourteenth day, they crossed the North Platte River. Eli looked at Charlie as they came from the water and their horses shook the water off, and Eli grinned. "You've prob'ly heard 'em say that the North Platte is too thick to drink and too thin to plow! Now you know why!" As they moved away from the water and the trees, the well-traveled road of the Oregon Trail showed itself, lying in the shadow of the new railroad of the Union Pacific. They kept to the road, turned to the west and headed across the western end of Nebraska.

They rode into the setting sun, watching the dancing lights and colors of the sunset as the golden orb slowly lowered itself to the western horizon. Long lances of gold stretched to the highest reaches of the blue sky, brilliant hues of orange and red painted the remaining clouds that hung lazily in the western sky, and the colors seemed to melt onto the land about them, giving an added richness of color to the dry land of the flats where flat-top buttes and jagged edged mesas stood lonesome off their right shoulders and the distant pillars of stone marked the western lands of Nebraska.

Eli grinned, glanced to Charlie to see a smile on his face, and looked back at the colorful display of God's welcome to the west. Eli said, "Yo! I see some trees yonder, must be near water, maybe that'd be a good place to make our camp. And if you're a good Indian, you might shoot us somethin' for supper!" He chuckled, glancing to Charlie who was shaking his head and grinning.

CHAPTER 27

FRIENDS

Rusty's cold muzzle brought Eli instantly awake. It was not often that the big stallion would waken Eli in this way, usually it would be with a stomping foot, a deep-chested nicker, or just the common sense the two shared and felt when one or the other was alarmed. Eli did not move his head, just his eyes, as he looked about the camp, trying to see what he could by the light of the moon and starlit night, but when he heard shuffling, rumbling, and began to feel the movement of the ground, he sat up, rifle in hand and came to his feet to go to the trees and have a better look around. Charlie had also come awake and stood near another tree, his shadow fading into the darker shadow of the trees.

"Smell 'em?" he asked without turning to look at Eli.

Eli's nostrils flared, and he chuckled to himself. "Buffalo!" he declared.

The men spoke in low tones as they watched the thick dark blanket move across the sage and greasewood flats.

"And where there's buffalo, there's natives!" added Charlie.

"Didn't expect to see buffalo this time of year," commented Eli.

"Goin' south for the winter," stated Charlie. "But soon's it's light, one of 'em won't be goin' any further south."

"It'll be work, but it'll be worth it. That's good eatin'. So long as we don't attract some Sioux or Cheyenne that want it more'n we do."

It was not a big herd, maybe a couple hundred, but they were fat from feeding on the green grass in the north. This was the way of the great bison herds, come north in the spring, return south in the late fall, and it was this migratory manner that the natives lived by and made their tribal hunts, often moving whole villages to follow the herds. This herd was following the water of the North Platte River and would probably continue south into Kansas and Indian Territory, perhaps even into Texas.

As they watched the lumbering herd, the grey light of early morning began to split the darkness in the east and figures began to take form. They could see the rambunctious orange-hued calves running beside their mothers, kicking up their heels and racing with one another. Some old bulls were moving off to the side, watchful of the herd but avoiding the rowdy youngsters.

Charlie was eyeing the herd but also looking around and behind the herd for any followers. He turned to look around the trunk of the spindly cottonwood and nodded in the direction of the rear of the herd. "Get your glasses and have a look back there. Looks like it might be hunters."

Eli stepped to his saddle and saddlebags, retrieved

the binoculars and returned to the edge of the trees, lifted the glasses and scanned the flats behind the herd. The dust was heavy, but the morning dew had made less of it, and the cool morning breeze helped to dissipate the clouds enough so he could make out a handful of riders, but it did not look like a village or a hunting party, more like a family. He counted two men, or a man and a youth, mounted and one holding a lance, the other a bow, a woman, also mounted, and a grey-haired old man aboard a horse that appeared to be about as old. Another woman led a horse with a travois, and two or three youngsters nearby.

Eli lowered the glasses and looked to Charlie. "Looks to be a lone family, an old man, another man and a younger one, couple women, kids, travois. Musta got separated from the village or somethin'." He lifted the binoculars again. "They don't appear to have any rifles, just a bow and a lance, but they look mighty hungry! They're talkin', gesturin' to the herd, dunno what they're gonna do."

Eli lowered the glasses, reached for his Spencer and lifted it as he leaned against the tree for a brace, but before he could shoot, Charlie asked, "What'chu gonna do?"

"Gonna take a couple buffalo, share with the family, make friends." He grinned and looked at Charlie. "You traded that Henry for a Spencer, so you'd have a bigger gun, so use it!"

Charlie lifted his just as Eli dropped the hammer on his Spencer and a young bull drove his chin into the ground. The first shot did not spook the herd, they were not afraid of much of anything, but when three more animals dropped, the herd picked up its pace and began to churn the ground with their hooves as they hastened their southward bound travels.

Eli looked at Charlie. "You go ahead and get started, I'm gonna go get acquainted and see if they're hungry for some fresh meat." He began saddling the claybank, stepped aboard, slipped the Spencer into the scabbard and headed out of the trees toward the family. As he approached, he called out, "Aho! I'm friendly," holding his open palm high and facing the people.

The two men turned their ponies toward Eli and nudged them forward, the grey-haired oldster just frowning but not hesitating to come forward even without a weapon in hand. The second man who appeared to be a mature warrior, held his lance point forward, scowling at their visitor, yet neither man spoke. Eli reined up and motioned over his shoulder. "We shot some buffalo, I saw you had no rifles, so we shot three for your family." Eli used sign language as he spoke, and the men readily understood.

The old man grinned, nodded, and said, "Good, good. We need the meat."

He spoke in English, and Eli grinned, glad he was understood. He motioned them to follow and reined Rusty around and started back to their camp, a quick glance over his shoulder showed the family was following, but not closely. Eli rode directly to the first bull he had downed where Charlie was already splitting it from brisket to tail, stepped down and pushed up his sleeves to start helping. He watched the family come near, motioned them to the other carcasses, and dropped to one knee beside their bounty and helped Charlie. They field dressed the bull, pulling its entrails out and away, then began peeling back the hide until the top side was laid bare, then Eli mounted up, tossed the loop of his riata to Charlie who dallied it around the legs of the beast, then with a dally around his saddle horn, Eli turned Rusty away and dug his heels into Rusty's ribs to make the horse lean into the pull and roll the big bull over so they could finish skinning and deboning the bull.

When Eli and Charlie finished their work, they knew there was much left of the carcass that the family could use and they walked to the first carcass where the younger man, one of the women, and the older boy were busy at the butchering. Eli began to speak, using sign, and told of the liver, heart, and hide of their bull was theirs also, if they wanted it. The woman nodded her head smiling, and looked at her man as if there was something he was supposed to say.

He nodded, looked at the two and began. "We are thankful for the meat, and my woman would like for you to take a meal with us later." He spoke in English but appeared to say what he did, not because he wanted to, but because he was obligated.

Eli glanced to a grinning Charlie and said, "We would be honored to share a meal with you."

Charlie looked at their work, turned to look at the other carcass where the rest worked, and spoke in Lakota. "Are you Brulé or Oglala?"

The man frowned, and answered, "*Sičháǧu* Brulé!" proudly, lifting his shoulders and chin.

"Where is the rest of your village?" asked Charlie.

"We lost many to the white man's spotted disease. Our village divided, fled from the disease. The people in the wagons brought the spotted sickness," he grumbled, his anger evident.

Charlie translated to Eli, explained about the pox, and turned back to the man. "I am Charlie Two Toes and this"—motioning to Eli—"is Elijah McCain, Eli."

The man stood, blood up to his elbows, but motioned to himself. "I am Spotted Tail, he"—pointing to the old man—"is my father, Tangle Hair, and the woman is my mother, Walks-with-the-Pipe. My woman is Black Lodge, our daughter, Fallen Leaf, helps my mother."

Charlie pointed to the trees. "Our camp is there, when you are ready, come to our camp and make your place. We will leave in the morning."

Spotted Tail nodded and turned back to his work as Eli and Charlie started back to the camp, their horses loaded heavy with the meat from the bull. While Eli unloaded, Charlie went to the river's edge and cut an armload of willows to make drying racks for much of the meat. They would cut it into thin strips, hang it on the rack over smoking coals, and let it smoke through the night. It would provide meat for the two of them for many days. They had just finished with their racks when the others came into the ample clearing with their gear and the women set about erecting the hide lodge while the men gathered firewood and willows for them to make racks like Charlie and Eli, but some of their meat would be made into pemmican and they would stay in this camp while the women gathered the harvest of berries to blend with the meat. But when the lodge was raised, the women set about preparing their meal to share with their new friends.

CHAPTER 28

WAGONS

W alks-with-the-Pipe, Black Lodge, and Fallen Leaf were exceptionally industrious as they fixed the evening meal, readied much of the meat for smoking, and started the process for smoking the meat, preparing pemmican, and tending to the lodge to make a comfortable camp for their family. They were open and friendly, attentive to their visitors and excellent cooks. Eli and Charlie had not eaten their fill so satisfactorily in a long time and it was with considerable regret they packed their gear and readied to take to the trail with first light.

But first light saw them on the trail of the oft-traveled Oregon Trail and wagon road. The road continued to the south side of the North Platte River across Nebraska Territory, or what was now known as the state of Nebraska. It was flat country, populated by antelope, coyote, wolves, bobcat, a few lynx, an occasional black bear, and buffalo, but this was also the hunting grounds of the Lakota, Arapaho, Pawnee and more. The ruts of the road had been cut deep and wide, but the hot summers had flattened most of the ruts that had been carved over the last fifty years of settlers coming west to the Promised Land. All along the trail there were markers of their passing, from castoff furniture and other household goods to graves and the skeletons of butchered buffalo, deer, and worn-out oxen and horses. These were monuments to the determination and grit of a people that yearned to be free and independent, tired of taskmasters and turmoil of wars, families by the hundreds sought nirvana in the plains and mountains of the West.

Eli and Charlie continued west until it was late in the day on the second day out from their time with the Brulé, when they came to a group of circled-up wagons that sat in the shadow of what was known as Courthouse Rock and Jailhouse Rock. The sun was lowering behind the unusual rock formations and painting the sky with golds, oranges, and yellows in a grand display of a kaleidoscope of colors, all of which lay on the land like a homespun quilt of many colors.

Eli and Charlie rode toward the wagons and called out a greeting, "Hello the camp! Mind if we come in?"

Two swarthy men stepped from between the wagons, both holding rifles across their chests as they looked at the two visitors. One man nodded. "Come on in, if'n you're friendly. Keep your hands clear of your weapons, and welcome." As they neared, the speaker added, "I'm Carl Hughes, and this is Howard Jones, step down, friend."

"Thanks, and I'm Elijah McCain and this is Charlie Two Toes," at the name of Charlie, the big man frowned, looked at Charlie with one eyebrow cocked high, and asked, "You an Injun?"

Charlie did his best to remain stoic and answered, "Ugh. Me Pawnee."

Eli laughed. "Don't pay any attention to him, he's only half Pawnee, the rest is clown! He can talk English better'n most of us." He shook his head as he grabbed the lead of Rusty and Grey and started into the circle of wagons. Several others came near, each extending a hand to greet the newcomers and giving their names, but there were too many for Eli to remember them all until a tall husky man with greying hair and a black frock coat that showed a little wear at the sleeves and collar, and with blue eyes that danced with interest and friendliness as he introduced himself. "Welcome friends. We're glad to have you with us. I'm Parson Shadrach Spencer. Will you men be with us on the morrow?"

"Don't rightly know, Parson, we're just travelin' through."

"Well, don't be in a big hurry. Tomorrow is the sabbath, and we'll be having services here in the circle and you men are certainly welcome to join us."

"Might just do that, Parson. We don't often get the chance to attend worship services," answered Eli, shaking the man's hand.

Carl Hughes stepped forward and touched Eli's elbow. "Uh, my family would like to invite the two of you to join us for supper, if you're of a mind."

"We would be honored, but we were going to make our camp down there"—nodding toward the creek that lay below the wagons—"and if we'd have time, we'd like to tend to our animals first."

"Oh, certainly." He reached into the small pocket of his leather vest, pulled out a watch, and said, "Shall we say seven thirty?"

"That'd be fine, Carl. Uh, we have some fresh meat if that would help?"

"I'm sure it would, although I don't know exactly what my wife is fixing," he answered with a grin.

Eli went to the panniers aboard the grey, pulled out a sizable rump roast, and handed it over to Carl. "That's buffalo, if you've not had any before, it should be a treat."

"Buffalo? That *will* be special. Thank you. I'll get this to Elaine right away. We'll see you soon!" he declared as he started down the line of wagons to deliver the delicacy.

It did not take them long to set up their camp and tether the horses within reach of graze and water. The little creek meandered through the willows and cottonwoods and made the camp all the more comfortable with the cool fresh water at hand. The men freshened up and returned to the wagons a little less dusty and considerably cleaner, hair combed, and broad smiles splitting their faces when they smelled all the aromas of the different suppers cooking. Carl met them at the break in the wagons and escorted them back to their family wagon to introduce them.

"Men, this is my wife, Elaine, my son, Robert, and daughter, Samantha. And this is my sister, Meaghan."

They were greeted by smiles all around, nods, and a slightly embarrassed sister whose golden tresses cascaded over her shoulders and her bright blue eyes kept looking at Charlie and he could not take his eyes off Meaghan. She appeared to be all of twenty-five, very pretty and with a figure that could only be described as voluptuous. Elaine was dark-haired, slender, dark-brown eyes, and dimples with a radiant smile that included everyone in its warmth. Robert was about twelve, curious, with an unruly mop of hair that hid his forehead and got in his eyes prompting him to brush it away or shake his head to move the hair aside. His somber expression showed one of interest and intent, a young man determined to grow up into manhood in a hurry.

The girl was about nine, dark hair, freckles that marched across her nose and cheeks above the dimples, and a timid manner that kept her close by her mother's side. Carl was also blonde, blue-eyed, about six foot tall, broad-shouldered, confident manner and friendly, but cautious.

Elaine spoke up. "I was so pleased with the meat you provided. It was too big a cut to get ready for supper, but I cut it into thinner slices, simmered it, and smothered it in gravy. I've already had a bite and it is tender and tasty, thank you so much!"

They were all seated around a long plank table. Carl asked the Lord's blessing on the meal, and the group began to get acquainted. Carl asked Eli, "So, you men been on the trail long?"

"Oh, couple weeks. We were down in Indian Territory, scouting for the cavalry. Now we're just headin' to the mountains."

Elaine asked, "Don't you have families?"

Charlie answered, "I don't, never seemed to stop long enough to get married!" He chuckled. "Met up with him" —nodding to Eli—"in California, drove a herd of horses across country to Fort Hays, started scouting, then…" He shrugged and accepted the offered bowl of potatoes.

Elaine looked to Eli. "And you, Eli?"

Eli grinned. "Yes and no. I was married, we had twin sons, but I was in the Union Cavalry during the war, spent a lot of time apart, and when I returned, my wife passed, my sons went west, and I had made a promise to my wife to try to find them and get them to return home, so I set out on a search that took most of a year and crossed this wide country before I found them, and they returned to the family home in Kentucky to get married and begin their families."

"You were in the cavalry?" asked Carl.

Eli nodded and reached for his coffee cup to take a sip.

"What rank were you?"

"Lieutenant Colonel under General Phil Sheridan."

"You sound like an educated man…"

"West Point."

"Are you familiar with this part of the country?" asked Carl.

"I was stationed at Fort Laramie for a few years, got well acquainted with this country and the people of the land." He paused, took another sip of coffee, set the cup down, and continued. "But enough about me, what brought you folks to the West?"

Elaine dropped her eyes and mumbled, "Gold."

Carl chuckled. "Well, it's more than that. We had a farm in Missouri, but a couple years of drought, a plague of locusts, fire, one thing after another and before we knew it, we were about bankrupt, and then we heard of the wagon train that was forming to go west, most talkin' about Montana territory and the gold fields, and it seemed like the best possibility for a new start. So we joined up and here we are." He looked about, "And that's about the same or similar story for most of these folks, oh, there are a couple that are only interested in gettin' to the gold fields, but some of us are looking at land and such all the way along."

"Who's your wagonmaster?"

Carl dropped his eyes. "About that," he began. "He,

the wagonmaster and his scout, were two of those that were just interested in getting to the gold fields and I reckon he considered it safer to travel with a wagon train, than by themselves. We had a couple visitors a few days back that gave the news about the Bozeman Trail being closed and no wagons allowed, how the Indians were burning all the forts and such, and Smitty, the wagonmaster, and his scout slept on it, and were gone the next morning. That was yesterday."

"So, what are you going to do now?" asked Eli.

Carl looked at Eli, Charlie, then to his wife and family, dropped his eyes to the table and lifted them again, looked intently at Eli "Would you consider…"

CHAPTER 29

CONGREGATION

"But what do you think we should do?" asked a matronly woman who stood with arms crossed and her long apron blowing in the wind.

It was early morning, and everyone had finished their breakfast and at the insistence of Carl Hughes and a few of the other men who had risen to the temporary leadership positions, they gathered near Carl's wagon, and he had introduced Eli and Charlie. Carl had introduced the as men familiar with the country and might be of help to the stranded train.

When the woman asked the question that seemed to be on everyone's mind, Eli stepped forward, looking at the people, seeing a typical crowd of settlers that would have been much the same on any of the hundreds of trains that had traveled this very trail. He began with, "First off, folks, we're heading into winter, and winter is the last time that you want to try to take a wagon train through the mountains."

A face full of whiskers above a barrel chest stepped up and said, "Winter is winter, ain't no different. Snow is cold, white an' wet. I don't see why we can't take our wagons through!"

Eli dropped his eyes to the ground, lifted them to look at the complainer directly. "First off, winter is not winter. Unless you've experienced winter in the Rocky Mountains, you've never experienced winter. The temperature can get fifty below zero, sometimes worse'n that, the snow will pile up to fifteen feet to twenty feet, and drift up to fifty feet deep, sometimes deeper. A bad storm could bury your entire train and it wouldn't be found until well after spring thaw. You and your horses could go snow blind, freeze to death or be like the Donner party that crossed the Sierras and ended up freezing and eating each other. Now, some of the youn-gun's might be tender and tasty, but from the looks of you, ain't nobody gonna want a bite!" The crowd laughed, and Eli continued, "There is another way north to the goldfields of Montana, it was the Bozeman Trail that was closed, it followed part of the Bridger Trail, then started north on a different route. The Bridger Trail is still open, it's a more difficult trail, steeper climbs, not as good a road, but it'll get there. But...not until spring."

"So, like I said afore, what do you think we should do?"

"I think the smart thing would be to winter at or near Fort Laramie, get fresh supplies in the spring and head north on the Bridger, or you could go further west to Salt Lake area and then north, but that's about two weeks to a month further."

"Have you been to the goldfields?" asked another.

"I have."

"What part?"

"Virginia City, Helena, Last Chance Gulch, Bear Gulch." He shrugged.

"How's come you didn't stay?"

"Not a gold miner."

At that answer, Shadrach Spencer stepped forward, turned to face the crowd. "That's enough for now folks, go on an' get your chairs an' such, we're gonna have our worship service here right soon now."

The crowd turned away, talking among themselves, and did as the parson had bidden. He turned to Eli. "You gonna join us for worship, Sonny?"

Eli grinned. "Certainly, Parson. Wouldn't miss it. I'll go fetch my Bible and be right back."

At the mention of getting his Bible, the parson grinned and nodded. "Good, good."

———

The parson stood before the people, and with an upright shipping box serving as a makeshift pulpit before him. Somber faced he looked about the crowd, silence fell over them as eyes dropped and people fidgeted under the wilting gaze of the seasoned pulpiteer. His deep voice came softly as he began. "Folks, in case you haven't figgered it out, we are in what some would call a pickle, a jam, an' I'm not talkin' 'bout lunch!"

Many chuckled but the parson continued. "Ofttimes the Lord allows us to go 'bout our own ways just so we will get in just such a predicament that makes us turn back to Him. So, this mornin' I'd like us to look to the book of Psalms for some encouragement and guidance. Psalm 25 verses 1 through 5 *Unto thee, O Lord, do I lift up my soul. O my God, I trust in thee: let me not be ashamed, let not mine enemies triumph over me. Yea, let none that wait on thee be ashamed: let them be ashamed which transgress without cause. Show me thy ways, O Lord; teach me thy paths. Lead me in thy truth, and teach me: for thou art the God of my salvation; on thee do I wait all the day.*

The parson began with a short prayer asking for God's guidance and the Spirit's leading. When he said "Amen" and lifted his eyes to the crowd. "We've been fussin' and worryin' for a couple days now and some of us have been prayin' and askin' the Lord to show us what we oughta be doin'. I went a little further and asked, 'Lord, we don't know what we're doin' or where we're goin' so I reckon we'll be needin' you to send us someone who does.' And maybe He's done just that." He looked around at the crowd, stepped from behind the pulpit, rested his arm on the box, and began. "Now among a crowd like this, we have all sorts of excuses or reasons for bein' on this hyar journey. Some are just lookin' for a new home, a new start, a new beginning. Some are so et up with greed and lust you're wantin' to find gold so you can get rich an' buy ever'thin' you want. But whatever the reason, we're in this together, and we can't be just relyin' on our reckonin' to get us where we need to be goin'. Our text tells us to *trust.* That means to let our God lead us and not be goin' on our own way. We are to go to Him and ask Him to *show me thy ways, O Lord, teach me thy paths.* Then it says to *Lead me in thy truth and teach me for thou art the God of my salvation.* Now, I wanna park there a moment, if'n you don't mind. *The God of my salvation…*salvation, to be saved, delivered from Hell and damnation." He paused, looking around at the scenery, the big rimrock butte that stood like an ancient castle that was called Courthouse Rock and the smaller one that stood just as tall and was called Jailhouse Rock.

"These monoliths are called Courthouse and Jailhouse. Kinda poignant, don't you think? Here we are in the middle of what seems like nowhere, abandoned by our guide, tryin' to figger things out on our own, and it's kinda like we're bein' judged at the courthouse and threatened by the jailhouse. Why? Because we haven't been dependin' on God, that's why. It all begins with His salvation. So let me ask you a question. If the wild Indians of this land were to swoop down on us today and kill ever one of us, what happens then? Huh? You goin' to Heaven or Hell? Or do you know? You see my friend it all starts with *His* salvation, and if you've never accepted God's wonderful gift of salvation, you're destined for an eternity without Him. So, that's what we need to settle first. Now…" He paused, took a deep breath, and continued. "This chapter 25 of Psalms tells us all we need to know. First thing is to know we're all sinners and because of that, the penalty is death and hell forever. But God does not want that for us so He says He'll show us the way, verse 8, and will forgive us if we ask Him, verse 11 and 18, and we will receive his covenant or promise of eternal life, verse 14, so if we put our trust in Him, He will deliver us, verse 20, and deliver us out of our troubles."

He paused again, took a deep breath and stepped back behind his pulpit and continued, "So, if there has never been a time in your life when you have turned from your sins, asked for God's forgiveness, trusted Him to give you that gift of eternal life to make sure of Heaven, then now's the time." He paused, looking at the crowd, many with upturned faces, waiting. "If you mean it with all your heart, then repeat this prayer after me, but don't do it unless you believe it and mean it. 'Dear God, I want to trust you today to forgive me of my sins, come into my heart and cleanse me, and give me that gift of eternal life, your salvation, so that I will know Heaven as my eternal home. Thank you, God. I pray this in Jesus's name. Amen."

The "Amens" were heard throughout the crowd and faces were uplifted, many with tears in their eyes and smiles on their faces. And the parson continued. "Wonderful, wonderful. Now we can go to verse four, *Show me thy ways, O Lord; teach me thy paths*. And together, we can trust the Lord to give us the guidance to get to where He would have us to go."

He chuckled, looked around and added, "Now let us ask the Lord's blessing on the food!"

He prayed a short prayer of thanksgiving and for the Lord's blessing on the days to come, and finished with, "...and all the people said," and the others joined him, and the entire crowd said together, "AMEN!"

When the parson stepped away from his pulpit, he went directly to Eli and asked, "So, my son, are you going to help us out of this situation?"

Eli chuckled. "That will depend on what the people say, Parson. If they're in agreement and want me and Charlie to help, we'll do just that. But I'll not be leading anyone into the mountains to get buried in a snowdrift or an avalanche. If they want to wait it out at Fort Laramie, then we'll do what we can."

"Good, good," responded the parson, his smile splitting his face beneath bright eyes.

CHAPTER 30

BLUFFS

The shadows were stretching long behind them, and the western skies were parading their colors to announce the end of another long day. Charlie was well out front, scouting, but he was not alone, Carl's sister, Meaghan, had mounted her own buckskin and rode out to side Charlie, even though he voiced his concern, he did not complain. Eli was out front of the wagons and both Carl and his son, Robert, were riding with him.

"The sunsets in this country are nothing short of magnificent," declared Carl, shading his eyes to the glare of the sun. He wore a flat-brimmed felt hat, and his son was the spitting image of his father, dressed similar, same hat, and his physical features showed him to be molded in the image of his father.

"Wait till you see them in the mountains," offered a grinning Eli. "All those colors seem to lay on the snow-capped mountains and paint them as mirror images of the sky."

"I imagine that would be somethin' to see," replied

Carl. "But it seems every part of the country we cross has its own marvels, like that"—pointing off their left shoulder—"that thing sticking up in the middle of nowhere. Ain't that sumpin'?"

Eli grinned. "That's Chimney Rock, looks like a chimney from something down below."

"What's that one behind it, it looks like Jailhouse Rock, but different," inquired Robert, pointing to the west beyond Chimney Rock.

"Don't know if it's got a name, just another clay and sandstone upthrust. That long round-topped ridge yonder doesn't have a name either, leastways, not that I know. But it does make a good lookout to see what's goin' on around hereabouts."

"You expectin' somethin'?" asked Carl, frowning.

"Always expect somethin'," answered Eli. "It's when you don't expect it that it gets you."

"What gets you?" asked Robert.

"Oh, just 'bout anything. Storms, both dust storms and rain or snow, breakdowns, flash floods, Indians, outlaws, you name it, we're in the wilderness and anything could happen."

"Indians? You think we could run into Indians?" asked Robert, excited and leaning forward to see past his father to Eli.

"Haven't you had any run-ins with Indians before this?" asked Eli, frowning as he looked at Carl.

"No, we've seen them at a distance, the wagonmaster said they were peaceful Pawnee, but other'n that, none."

Eli shook his head. "Then you're almighty blessed or lucky or both. The Cheyenne, Arapaho, Lakota, Kiowa, and even some Comanche, have all been raiding through the plains the last several months. There have been hundreds of settlers, freighters, soldiers, families, that have been burned out, and wiped out, just between Topeka and Fort Laramie. And that's in the last six months or so. This train has Thirty-seven wagons, and by most standards, that's a small train. The natives would know right off that you don't have more'n fifty or sixty fighting men and they often field more'n a hundred, sometimes two hundred warriors in a raiding party."

"Have you fought Indians, Eli?" asked Robert.

"Sure have, Robert."

"Recently?"

"All too many times, all the way from California to Kansas to Indian Territory and here in Nebraska."

"Kill any of 'em?"

"Yes, Robert, but only when I had to. You see, the natives are people just like us. Oh, they don't have wagons and such, but they have families, boys and girls like you and your sister, and their homes are called lodges, or tipis. They're made out of buffalo hide and are quite comfortable, and when they want to move, they take 'em down, put them on a travois, and go where they want. The father and mother love their children just like your mom and dad love you, and they teach them what they need to learn to have a good life. They were here in this land, long before the white man came and now they fight to keep their homes, just like you and your father would fight to keep yours."

He paused, waved his arm around to take in all the land around them. "This used to be the land of the Cheyenne people, they lived here, hunted here, grew up and died here. Then came the Arapaho and the Lakota and the Pawnee, they all fought over the hunting land, because the buffalo herds come through here going north in the spring, and back to the south in the fall. They depend on the buffalo for just about everything they have. They use the hides for their lodges, the sinew for sewing, the hooves for glue, the horns for cups, the bones for plates, and more. But now the white man wants to kill them all for their hides and leave the meat to spoil. That's why the natives are angry and want to drive the white man from this land."

"Gee, I didn't know all that," mumbled a somber Robert. He turned to look at his dad. "Did you, Pa? Did you know all that?"

"Just a couple days ago we were visiting with a family of Brulé Lakota. We shared our kills of buffalo with them. They told us how the white man's spotted disease almost wiped out their whole village."

"Spotted disease?" asked Robert.

"Smallpox."

"Oh," answered Robert, then lifting his eyes to Eli. "You shared your buffalo kills with them?"

"We did. When we saw they had no rifles and the buffalo herd was passing, we shot a couple extra so we could help them out. They need the meat to last through the winter, otherwise they might starve. Doesn't the Bible tell us, *inasmuch as ye have done it unto one of the least of these my brethren, ye have done it unto me?*"

"Gee, I don't know if I could do that," replied Robert. "How 'bout'chu, Pa?"

"Well, I don't know, Robert. I've never had that opportunity."

Eli had reined up, shaded his eyes as he looked to the southwest beyond the point of rimrock buttes to the south of the trail. They were a few miles past Chimney Rock, and this line of buttes offered more cover to an attacking horde if they were to move against the wagons. He reached into his saddlebags and brought out his binoculars and stood in his stirrups to look to the distance. He sighed heavily, dropped into the seat of his saddle. "You might have that opportunity sooner'n you'd like. Let's go back to warn the wagons."

"Warn the wagons?" asked Carl, alarm showing on his face as he glanced from Eli to Robert.

Eli answered, "'Bout those Indians yonder."

He reined Rusty around and started back to the wagons at a lope, Carl and Robert close behind. As they neared the wagons, he made the sign to circle up and shouted, "Circle up! Circle up! Now!" and watched as the wagons began to form the circle of defense. As the men were unhitching their teams, Eli and Carl rode into the circle, stripped the gear from their mounts and Eli went around the wagons preparing the people. "If you have the weapons, arm your women and any others that can shoot. If not, you ladies find cover and reload the weapons for the men."

"What about muh young'uns?" asked one man, nodding to three youngsters in their early teens or close.

"If you have the weapons, put 'em to work!" answered Eli. He went to the center of the circle and called out, "Listen up, folks!"

When they turned their attention to him, he continued.

"These are Cheyenne Dog Soldiers, they are some of the fiercest fighting men in the Indian nations. When you take aim, you aim to kill, if you don't, they will take two or three bullets and keep coming and they'll kill you, take your scalp, mutilate your body, take your women and children and do the same. You are fighting for your lives! Don't forget that!" He looked around at the different people. "Pick your targets, don't get in a hurry, squeeze off your shots."

Carl stepped beside him, and in a low voice, asked, "Have you seen Charlie and Meaghan?"

"No, but he'll take care of her, don't worry. There's not a man I'd rather be with in a tight situation than Charlie."

Eli climbed up on the seat of a nearby wagon, shaded his eyes and looked in the direction of the rolling hills where he had seen the warriors. A dust cloud rose into the fading light catching the colors of the sunset and told of the nearness of the warriors.

"They're coming," he said, just loud enough for Carl to hear. "But they're in no hurry."

"I thought Indians didn't fight after dark," offered Carl.

"They fight whenever they think they can win and get some plunder. Some don't fight after dark, but you can't count on that."

CHAPTER 31

CONFRONTATION

"How far ya' reckon?" came the question in a familiar voice.

Eli turned to see a grinning Charlie standing beside the wagon, looking up at his friend.

"When'd you get back?" asked Eli.

"Just a bit ago, time enough to help with the wagons an' such." He stepped to the front of the wagon, shaded his eyes for his own look-see. "Dog Soldiers, eh?"

"Looks like."

"Might be the same bunch that's been raidin' hereabouts. We came onto three farms that were hit, burned out, ever'body kilt. Probably twenty or so, din't take time to bury 'em, thot we oughta come back, what with the girl an' all."

"She sees it all?"

"Yup, got sick 'bout it too…" He paused and shook his head. "Wimmin!"

Eli chuckled. "They got their good side too."

"You betcha." Charlie chuckled. "She do!" He looked at Eli.

"But what about the Cheyenne?"

"Doesn't look like we need to worry 'bout them tonight, they look to be makin' camp below that butte yonder," stated Charlie, pointing to the nearest rimrock butte.

Eli looked and nodded. "'Pears so," and began climbing down from the wagon. He looked at Charlie. "You keep your eye on 'em, I'm gonna talk to the folks, maybe have 'em get some supper an' such."

As he walked among the people, he spoke. "Ladies, you go ahead and fix your supper, but when it comes to eatin'"—he turned to the men that stood by the wagons —"alternate wagons for the men to take time to eat. Then make up your beds and we'll do the same, alternate getting some sleep and standing guard. We'll need to do that until sunup, then we'll see what we need to do."

As he walked the circle, Eli was pleased to see the people had been gathering buffalo chips and any possible firewood as they passed and tossed it into the hammock of a blanket that hung under the wagons. No one would have to leave the circle to gather firewood for the cook-fires, at least not tonight.

The long night was silent and still, the usual cool night breeze had abandoned the lonely wagons, the parson was making the rounds, talking, encouraging, praying with the people. Charlie came alongside Eli who stood at the end of a wagon, watching the shadows of the night, trying to pierce the darkness with his limited vision. He had carefully preserved his night vision by avoiding all the cookfires, keeping his back to the center of the circle, hoping to see any advance scouts of the Cheyenne before they came too near. The moon was waning from full and now showed about half its somber face, the dim blue light doing little to illuminate the flatlands with the numerous shadows of sage and grease-wood. The stars shone bright on the clear black velvet sky, but even the movement of the moon stretched the dim shadows of the flats, giving the appearance of movement, but nothing stirred. A couple of lonesome coyotes sang their sad tunes to one another, cicadas rattled their armor, crickets chattered, and the dry wood of the wagons seemed to creak even though they did not move.

Charlie came alongside, stood silent for a moment, then softly spoke. "I'm 'bout half-tempted to sneak out there 'mong 'em, put the fear of *Maheo* in 'em."

"*Maheo*?" asked Eli.

"Yeah, that's their name for their god, at least the one above. They got another'n down below but I dunno his name."

"You really think we could do it?"

"I prob'ly could, not too sure 'bout you." Charlie chuckled.

Eli looked at the stars. "It's after midnight, might be a good time if we was to do it."

"You can tell time by the stars?" asked Charlie, disbelieving.

"Nah," answered Eli, and held out his gold pocket watch to show Charlie.

Charlie grinned and shook his head. "White man!" he grumbled.

Eli flipped open the cover, held it out for Charlie to hear as it played a tune, and laughed at his response. Charlie shook his head, looked at Eli, and asked, "We goin'?"

"Yeah, lemme get my moccasins," he said, and he started to his packs, quickly returned with his Winchester Yellow Boy in hand and nodded for Charlie to take the lead. It was a little more than a mile to the camp of the Cheyenne, but with the tall sage and thick greasewood, they had to make a roundabout way to get near. Their camp had been made in the edge of the tree line of juniper that blanketed the flanks of the butte, and it offered good cover for the two men. They stopped just inside the trees, and Charlie whispered to Eli, "That watch important to you?"

Eli frowned. "Whadaya mean?"

"I was thinkin' if I could put it in the medicine pouch of the war leader, it might scare him, make him think he's lost his power. Does that thing go off reg'lar, you know, on the hour or just when you set it?"

"On the hour, plays for a minute, quits."

Charlie grinned. "Great, it'll scare the heebie-jeebies outta him and anyone around him." He dropped to a crouch, looking under and through the branches at the sleeping figures and for any sentries. He nodded toward a bigger tree. "There's a sentry. You take that'n, I'll take the one yonder," pointing to another tree near the picketed horses. "Then I'll go to the war leader, he's the one yonder, away from the others."

The men nodded to one another and started on their way, Charlie had further to go, and Eli wanted to get to his so he would not see Charlie and sound an alarm. It was only about forty to fifty feet, but he moved slow, crawling on his belly, watching every inch of the way and it took all of twenty minutes to go that far. Eli was behind the tree where the sentry sat, leaning against the tree and Eli could tell by the man's breathing, he was asleep. As his head bobbed forward, the warrior jerked back, looked around, and sat back.

Eli watched as the man's breathing resumed its regular rise and fall, his chin lowered to his chest, and Eli rose to a crouch. He reached around the tree, put his hand over the man's mouth and nose and slit his throat with the razor-sharp Bowie knife. The man kicked out, but his moccasins found nothing, and he slumped in death. Eli slowly released his grip on the man, held him against the tree, and when certain he was stable, Eli moved away into the darkness. His rifle was slung at his back, and he brought it around, loosed the sling, and held the rifle at the ready, finger on the trigger, thumb on the hammer. He had already jacked a shell in the chamber and all that was needed was to cock the hammer and let the bullet fly.

As Charlie made his way around the camp, he moved as silent as the night breeze, but on the way, he picked up a cone from a piñon tree, and some thin twigs from a sage. He was grinning as he planned what he would do, but slowly made his way to the second sentry. He moved as did Eli, coming at the man from behind and quietly caught him dozing, put his hand over his nose and mouth and the blade of his knife at his throat. He whispered into the man's ear, "What is the name of your war leader? If you tell me his name, I will let you live."

The man was wide-eyed and moved his eyes to see the man who held him tight, he nodded his agreement and Charlie slowly loosed his grip until the man whispered, "Lone Eagle"

Charlie nodded, flipped his knife until he held it by the blade and used the heavy haft to rap the man on the head, rendering him unconscious.

Charlie moved on his belly, inches at a time, and came alongside the war leader, rose up on his arms to look about and found the man's medicine bundle, lying between his shoulder and his head, the thong still around his neck. Charlie slowly lifted the bundle, pulled it open, and dropped the opened pocket watch within.

He pulled the drawstring tight, laid the bundle back, dropped his crafted figure from the pine cone and the twigs that was made to resemble a spider, the figure for *Maheo,* the Cheyenne name for the creator, and backed away into the darkness.

Charlie soon returned to Eli and the two men, grinning, nodded to one another and took off to the wagons at a trot. The moon was lowering in the west and the darkness was beginning to retreat from the coming dawn.

As they neared the wagons, Eli called out, "Don't shoot, it's Eli and Charlie," and trotted into the circle, bent over, hands on knees and fought for their breath.

When they stood erect, they looked at one another and started laughing. Eli shook his head, glanced to his friend and to Carl who stood, dumbfounded, and said, "We just went for a little look-see to our neighbors. You know, just bein' friendly."

"You went to the camp of the Indians?" asked Carl, Meaghan standing beside him, both looking somewhat stunned.

"We had an idea that might keep 'em from attacking. Might work, might not, we'll see pretty soon. It'll be full light in a short while," explained Eli, looking at the eastern light where the sun was sending out announcement of its arrival in the form of flame-colored lances that stretched across the sky. Eli climbed back to the seat of the nearest wagon, shaded his eyes to look to the butte that sheltered the Cheyenne, and saw movement. He turned to Charlie. "Hand me the binoculars, please," he said, and accepted them as Charlie lifted them to him.

"They're coming!" he declared, turned to look at Charlie, grinned. "The pulpit's yours!" and turned to trade places with Charlie.

CHAPTER 32

RIVER

Charlie stood on the seat of the wagon, stripped off his shirt, let his hair fall free and lifted his rifle over his head, holding it with both hands and watched as the raiding party of Cheyenne Dog Soldiers rode slowly forward. When they were within shouting distance, Charlie screamed his war cry, and shouted in the tongue of the Cheyenne, "Ho Lone Eagle, leader of the Dog Soldiers, I came to you last night, the image of *Maheo* that lay by your blankets was left there by me, Charlie Two Toes, known as Running Fox by my people the *Ckiiri* or Wolf People of the Pawnee. I could have easily killed you and sent you to *Maheo*, but I put magic in your medicine bundle that will remind you many times of my visit. If you are wise, you will take your warriors and return to your village, or you and all your warriors will die like Black Kettle and his woman, and his village died. Aiiiiieeeee!"

Lone Eagle had reined up and listened as Charlie spoke, looked about to his warriors and as he did, the chime of the watch in his medicine bundle began to sound and he screamed and grabbed at the bundle. He did not dare to throw it away for it held the special secret tokens of his medicine that he depended on to keep him alive in his time of war, but the sound was like nothing he had ever heard. The nearby warriors heard it also and their fear prompted the horses to become skittish and the mumbling, screaming, and shouting among the warriors sent fear through them all. Lone Eagle was confused, fearful, and dug heels to his mount and lifted his lance and shouted at his warriors and led them away to the southeast to round the east face of the big butte and disappear in a rising cloud of dust.

Charlie started laughing, bent over, hands on knees, and looked to Eli, grinning. "I ain't had so much fun in a coon's age!"

Eli grinned. "Just how long does a raccoon live, anyway?"

"Dunno, but it must be a long time. You ever tried to catch one?"

Eli chuckled, and the two men looked at the gathering crowd around them and Carl asked, "So, what'd you do?"

Charlie looked at Eli. Eli returned the stare, and both started laughing again. Eli turned back to Carl. "Oh, we just visited them last night, left 'em a little gift." He laughed, more of relief than humor, then explained, "Charlie snuck into their camp, slipped my pocket watch into the chief's medicine bundle, and apparently it started chiming the hour 'bout the time Charlie was talking. The 'spirit' in his bundle scared the chief and he thought his power was gone. When a warrior believes he has lost his power, he becomes very vulnerable and does not like to go to battle."

"Well, it sure beats having to fight 'em, that's for

sure," declared Meaghan, moving to Charlie's side and slipping her hand through the crook of his arm, smiling. Eli looked from Charlie to Meaghan and grinned, shook his head and turned away. He held his hands high, spoke to the people of the wagons. "Alright folks, let's get ready to move out, we've got four or five days till we get to Fort Laramie, then you can get all the rest you want!"

Charlie turned to Meaghan. "I'll be scoutin' out front, probably lookin' for some fresh meat, you wanna come along?"

Meaghan smiled, tugged on his arm, and answered, "Yes, yes I do. Shall I bring my rifle?"

"You've got a rifle?"

"I do, a Henry .44."

"Can you hit anything with it?" asked Charlie, frowning.

Meaghan smiled. "I can even hit a running target, even one that's running away!"

Eli chuckled, grinning at Charlie. "Bet she could prob'ly show you a thing or two about traps and snares, too."

The big bluff rose high above the valley floor, standing tall with broad shoulders, guarding the way of the North Platte as it came from the northwest and watered the flatlands that would one day be covered with bountiful farms. For now, it stood watch over the plains and the long jagged spine of a ridge that stretched back to the west as if pointing the way to the distant Rocky Mountains, while on it skirts that flared between the big buttes and the river, the dry land sprinkled with bunch grass, prickly pear, yucca, and cholla, was marred by the claw marks of the monstrous cloudbursts that could come, unannounced, and dig into the clay to leave behind the gnarled and jagged narrow

ravines, gullies, and gulches that would mar the land for
eons to come.

It was a clear day, the only clouds showing were dropping their shadows on the distant Black Hills in Dakota
territory, but the valley of the North Platte beckoned the
travelers westward and they followed the trail that sided
the south bank of the river. Stretching out on either side
were grasslands, bordered by rolling hills and beckoning
to men like Carl Hughes and his family that had been
seeking land where they could make a farm.

When the wagons stopped for the night, they made a
good camp near the river that offered good graze for the
horses and mules, protection from the wind with the
trees, and ample firewood for the cookfires. As usual,
Charlie and Eli made their camp apart from the others
and Charlie had cooking duties, but they were gladly
yielded to an eager Meaghan who had strip steaks
sizzling over the fire, because earlier they had bagged a
couple deer and shared the meat with the others, but
kept a loin for themselves. Now the coffee pot was
dancing on the stone slab beside the flames, and a dutch
oven was sitting cozy under the coals that covered the
top. Eli sat back and enjoyed watching the two chatter on
about nothing in particular, but just enjoying the
company of one another. Eli shook his head, recognizing
the signs of love in the eyes, laughter, and closeness of
the two. He was happy for Charlie who had often
expressed his thoughts that he would never find a
woman that would entice him to settle down, although
that was the chorus of every man until he met the
woman who baited her hook with just the enticement for
him to take it all, hook line and sinker! But Charlie was
certainly showing signs of dropping anchor. He guessed
that by the time springtime came and they had spent a

winter together, they would decide to spend every winter together after that.

As he watched the two, he reached for the coffee pot and poured himself a cup of the steaming brew, sat back and movement to his left caused him to turn and see Carl walking their direction. As he came into the firelight, he greeted them, "Evenin' folks." He looked to Eli, and asked, "Could I speak with you for a moment?"

"Of course, anything wrong?"

"No, nothing's wrong." He sat down on a flat rock and with elbows on his knees, hands clasped before him, he looked at Eli. "You know this country, right?"

"Some, yes, I've been here before."

"Several of us, the farmers, have been looking at this land we've been passing through and it looks good, good for farming. There's water, natural grasses, it's flat, well mostly, and there's trees to be used for lumber and building, it's mighty tempting."

"You mean tempting to make your home here?"

"Yes, that's what we've been thinking."

"Just you and your family, or are there more?"

"There's five wagons, five families, and we've been talking together about it."

"What about those burned-out farms we passed by today? And the ones Charlie and Meaghan told about? Just because the land is appealing, the neighbors not so much."

"We've thought about that, and we've talked about building a central stockade that if there was the threat of an attack, we could all make it to the stockade and defend ourselves together."

Eli nodded. "That's good thinking. And with five families, you might could make a go of it. Your nearest supply point would be Fort Laramie, and that's three, four days away, and that also means any help from the soldiers would be that far away."

Eli dropped his eyes, thinking about what the families were considering, knowing it was totally their decision and all they asked from him was his opinion, but the images of burned-out settlers, massacred natives, destroyed villages, were all fresh in his mind, and he did not want to come back this way and find these people in the same way. He glanced to Meaghan and Charlie, back to Carl. "What about Meaghan? What's she say?"

Carl grinned. "He and Meaghan said they would stay with us, help us and we would help them establish their home. Charlie said he'd like to give farming a try."

Eli grinned, shook his head, and glanced to his friend, who was totally focused on Meaghan as the two of them chattered on.

"Well, here's what I suggest you do. Talk to the parson, spend the night in prayer and thought, and if you still feel the same way tomorrow, then you can either come on to Fort Laramie with us, stock up for the winter, and return to start your homes, or, stay here, start your homes, and come to Laramie later on for more supplies. The rest of us will be camped there until spring."

Carl stood, grinning, extended his hand to shake with Eli, and walked back to the wagons, disappearing in the darkness.

CHAPTER 33

RAIDERS

When morning came, there was more than a foot of snow that lay heavy on the bedrolls and wagon bows. The deep cold pierced the blankets, coats, and bore into the very soul of the travelers. Eli walked into the circle, looking around at the slow-moving travelers, a few had their cookfires started, some huddled over steaming cups of coffee held tightly in cold fists, chins tucked deep into the collars, and feet stomping to get the blood flowing in their cold feet. It was a bitter awakening to the lateness of their journey, and Carl came to Eli's side. "We talked a bit, decided to go on to Laramie, spend the winter and come back in the early spring. We'd play hob tryin' to build cabins in this weather, and I don't suppose it'll get any better anytime soon."

Eli shook his head, shivered, and answered, "Prob'ly get worse 'fore it gets better. This part of the country, folks don't reckon the snow's deep till it's hip deep, an' it ain't cold till the thermometer breaks."

Carl shivered at the thought, looked at Eli, and asked, "Join us for breakfast?"

"Pleased to," he answered and followed Carl to his wagon where his wife, Elaine, was fussing over the cookfire. Meaghan saw Eli come near, looked past him with a question on her face, probably searching for Charlie. Eli smiled. "He'll be along soon, he's tendin' to the animals and gear."

Meaghan smiled, nodded, and turned to help her sister-in-law with the breakfast. By the time Charlie arrived, the ladies had started filling plates and serving their fixin's. The last of the strip steaks were smothered in gravy that covered fresh biscuits and sliced Indian potatoes harvested at their last campsite.

It was a tasty bounty, and the men especially enjoyed it on this cold morning. Elaine asked Eli, "How long 'fore we reach Fort Laramie?"

"Three, four days."

"Will this weather slow us down much?"

"Depends, if it stays cold, the ground will be hard and we can keep moving, but if it turns warm and turns this" —motioning to the snow—"into mud, then, yes, it will slow us down. But it's not too far and we'll be there 'fore you know it."

"Is the fort big, I mean, you know with stockade walls and such?"

"When I was first stationed there, it did have stockade walls, but it changed over time and there were as many buildings outside the walls as inside, more actually, so it kinda became a little village with several buildings, most out of adobe and stone. There's a good Post Traders store there that keeps well supplied and has just about anything you might need." He forked in a mouthful of food, enjoyed the steak and gravy, smiled, took a drink and continued. "The fort sits at the confluence of the North Platte and the Laramie rivers, and the Oregon Trail, the Mormon Trail, the Bozeman and the Bridger Trails all converge there, so it's usually a busy post. And that's not to mention the different native bands that often camp there. Sometimes you'll see Lakota, Sioux, Arapaho, Cheyenne, and more that have camps nearby."

"Oh my! Is it safe for us to camp that close to the Indians?" asked Elaine, straightening up and putting one hand on her hip, the other holding a big spoon she used to ladle the food with, as she looked wide-eyed at Eli.

Eli chuckled. "Oh, none of 'em would try anything with the soldiers nearby. Many of the natives that stay around there are called 'Loafer Indians' and just stay there for the annuities that are often paid out." He finished his coffee, stood and looked at Carl. "We best be getting a move on, we've a long way to go."

———

Eli lined out the wagons, putting the Hackworth wagon in the lead with their four-up of big mules to break trail, and the train made good time. It was early afternoon when they saw the black skeleton of a farmhouse and barn that even after the snowfall, a few wisps of smoke still curled heavenward. Eli and Charlie rode near, found the bodies of a man, a woman, and a young man, probably a son, spread-eagled on a fence behind the house with the remains of a fire having burned at their feet. The stench was stifling, and Charlie stepped down, grabbed a shovel from the pack aboard Grey, and started scraping away some snow to begin digging graves.

Eli said, "I'll get you some help," and turned back to the wagons.

Charlie looked up past the bodies and the remains of the barn, saw movement at the tree line, called out to Eli before he got too far, "Eli!"

Eli stopped, reined around, frowning and saw Charlie looking to the trees where several mounted warriors sat, watching, waiting. "C'mon, Charlie! Let's get back to the wagons, gotta warn 'em!"

Charlie swung aboard his buckskin and laying low on his neck, was soon beside the long-legged claybank as the two high-tailed it to the wagons. The Hackworths saw them coming, and Sebastian stood on his seat, looked behind them and motioned to the others to circle up! Sebastian Hackworth swung the big mules off the road and bent them around to start the circle, just as he heard the screaming war cries chasing Charlie and Eli. The two men skidded their mounts to a stop, hit the ground beside them, rifles in hand and laying the weapons across the seat of their saddles, they opened fire on the charging warriors. Their first volley took the two leaders, driving them to the ground off their mounts, and both men quickly jacked additional rounds into the chambers and took aim again. As fast as they could shoot, they sent bullets flying toward the charging and screaming warriors, but the screams of war cries soon changed, to shouts of fear and anger as six or seven of their fellow warriors lay dead on the roadway. One of the warriors that wore a hair-pipe bone breastplate, a tall porcupine roach, and three feathers in his hair, began shouting orders to the others and they turned their horses and retreated to the tree line further up the road.

As the wagons made their circle, the men had quickly unhitched the teams, brought them into the circle and

pulled the wagons closer, stacked anything and everything at hand in the spaces between the wagons, and had
taken their places, rifles at the ready, but none of the
warriors came near enough for them to get into the
fight.

Charlie and Eli looked at one another, stepped back
from their horses and led them into the circle, found a
box to sit on and breathing heavily, they looked around,
pleased at the fast-acting people that had made a good
circle for defense. Eli looked at some of the men nearby.
"Post some lookouts all around the circle, let the women
get some fires goin' and coffee on, we might be here a
bit."

Without a word, the men set about their duties, as
did the women and before long, Meaghan, with a broad
smile, brought two cups of steaming coffee to the two
friends that sat, gathering their strength and resolve. Eli
looked at Charlie, nodded to the blonde, and asked, "You
gonna marry that girl?"

"Thinkin' 'bout it." Chuckled Charlie. "She sure is
somethin', ain't she?"

"You could say that again." Eli chuckled.

"She sure is somethin', ain't she?" responded Charlie.
Eli frowned, looked at his friend who grinned and said,
"Well, you told me to say it again!" and laughed.

Eli shook his head and looked at his friend. "You
know we're goin' to have to go find those Cheyenne,
don'tchu?"

"Mmmhmm, I reckon."

Eli glanced at the sky. "Reckon we got three, maybe
four hours of daylight left, 'course that's just a guess,
mind you. If I had a pocket watch, I'd know for sure,
but..." He shrugged. Charlie glowered at his friend,
shaking his head, and said, "Mebbe we oughta get some

men to start digging those graves while we go huntin' trouble."

Eli nodded, stood, and went to Carl Hughes, explained what they were going to do and asked him to get a couple men and go dig the graves for the victims of the earlier raid by the natives. "I hate to ask, it's a gruesome detail, but it's the right thing to do," he explained. "You best take scarves to cover your nose and mouth with, it will be pretty rank."

Carl nodded. "I understand. We'll do it. What about the bodies of the Indians you killed comin' in?"

"Leave 'em. Usually they want to take the bodies back with 'em, but from what we could tell, that's a bunch of young bucks out to prove themselves. Just pull the bodies aside, but other'n that, leave 'em be."

"Well, you and Charlie take care and keep your heads down. It's no easy task you two have taken on, either." Eli nodded and returned to Charlie, and both men reloaded their rifles, stuffed some extra cartridges in their pockets, led their horses from the circle, checked the girths, and mounted up.

CHAPTER 34

FORT LARAMIE

The wagons made a few more miles after Eli and Charlie returned from their chase of the raiding party, and the clear blue sky and warm sun began to melt the snow and turn the road into a long bog of mud. Eli motioned for the wagons to circle up near the trees beside the river, knowing the grassy flats would support the wagons without making the road worse that what it already was, and he hoped for a cold night that would freeze the road, even though it would make the deep ruts harder to negotiate, it would be better and easier traveling than mud.

And it was a cold night, a bitter cold night, if they had a thermometer, it would easily register twenty to thirty below zero. The river had shown floating ice crystals and a thin sheet of ice near the banks before the sun tucked itself away. But now, the early morning light showed white from bank to bank. The horses and mules were slow moving, ice crystals at their nostrils and their eyelashes, and on their coats, and when the wagons started to move, even they groaned and complained. The grease at the axles so thick, it was hard to get the wagons moving, and when they did, the rattle of trace chains, the moans of the twisting wagons, and the groans of the wheels and axles, offered a symphony of trial and travail. The people wrapped scarves around their necks, lifted collars, pulled down hats, and still their breaths left traces of ice on their clothing. Men with mustaches and beards questioned the wisdom of forsaking shaving as the whiskers held icicles that dangled and moved with every breath, breaking off and dropping into their coffee cups and collars as they cradled the warm cups in their cold paws.

But the mules and horses leaned into their traces, dug deep at the hard frozen soil, and slowly began moving the wagon train. With the snow mostly gone, some of the people walked to give the animals relief at pulling the overloaded wagons, but the cold ground and icy air soon bit into their clothing and shoes, forcing them to ride and wrap extra blankets around their frost-bitten extremities. There was little talk, for each breath brought the sense of ice into their lungs and they preferred to keep their mouths and noses covered with the scarves, which silenced all conversation.

It was after the noon break, which was brief and offered only a couple fires to warm by, that the sun finally began to do its job of warming the countryside and giving relief to the cold figures among the wagons. The horses and mules moved more easily, their legs stretching out, and the wagons rolled without protest. By late afternoon, everyone was feeling better, and scarves were loosened, collars opened, and hats pushed back, and a few smiles began to show. Conversation could be heard, and even the youngsters were playing and laughing.

By nightfall, it was a tired group of people and animals that eagerly circled up for the nights camp. Warm fires blossomed and the fragrances of meals cooking filled the air, and folks walked about, talking with one another. They were surprised when they heard the clatter of many hooves on the roadway and looked to see the faces of uniformed men nearing the circle. The lights from the cookfires showing cold red cheeks above the blue uniforms and hungry eyes told the condition of the men.

Carl Hughes stepped forward. "Greetings, men. Won't you step down and join us? We don't have much, but what we have, we'll share."

A tall man moved his mount forward and stepped down. The captain's bars on his shoulder told of his leadership position and he removed his glove, offered his hand. "I'm Captain Smithers, out of Fort Laramie. We saw your fires, wanted to check on you folks."

"Why, thank you, Captain. Please, at least we can give you some hot coffee, maybe even a biscuit or two."

"That would be greatly appreciated, sir." He turned and nodded to the man behind him, a grizzled older man with first sergeant's stripes on his sleeve and several hash marks below that told of many hitches in the Army. The sergeant moved among the men. "Alright men, these fine folks have offered some hot coffee and biscuits, so step down and mind your manners."

Eli had come forward, shook hands with the captain, and asked, "You looking for something special, Captain?"

"We were told there were some raiding Indians down along the line, we rode out a ways to check on it."

"What'd you find?"

"Nothin', as usual. We get a lot of reports that are

just suspicions, some settler that's afraid of shadows..."
He shrugged.

Eli slowly nodded. "Been at the fort long?"

"Arrived last month. Came out from Jefferson
Barracks in Missouri."

Eli looked at the man and glanced to the weathered
first sergeant. "Well Captain, about your reports, we
passed several burned-out farms, slaughtered families,
and almost had a run-in with some Cheyenne Dog
Soldiers, and did have a running fight with a band of
young bucks from the Cheyenne just yesterday."

The captain stepped back and looked at Eli with a
frown of skepticism. "And just how do you know all this
about the natives?"

Eli chuckled, dropped his eyes. "We scouted for
Sheridan and Custer back in Indian Territory, before that
I was stationed here at Fort Laramie, and got to know
the natives pretty well."

"And your rank?"

"Lieutenant Colonel, Sheridan's cavalry at Appomattox and before that at Shenandoah."

Eli saw the first sergeant grinning and fighting to
keep from laughing, and a glance to the captain showed a
red-faced puffed-up junior officer who was out to make a
name for himself be it by deed or by bluster, at least he
was determined to prove himself.

The captain stuttered and stammered a moment, then
stood erect and said, "Well if that's the case, perhaps it
would be best if we accompanied your wagon train the
rest of the way into Fort Laramie."

"We would appreciate that, Captain. That's very good
of you." He stepped to the side and looked at the first
sergeant who was grinning and whose eyes were dancing
with mischief. "And as for you, First Sergeant O'Rourke,"

began Eli in a commanding voice. "Come here and shake my hand you ol' rascal you!"

The first sergeant gladly extended his meaty palm to Eli, wrapped the other arm around his shoulder and pulled him close. "Colonel, you are a sight for sore eyes, indeed you are!" The two old friends laughed and slapped one another on the shoulders and the sergeant asked, "So, where's your uniform, Colonel?"

Eli chuckled. "Oh, I left that behind a long time ago, somewhere about Appomattox."

The first sergeant sobered and looked at Eli. "Never thought I'd see the day, sir. You were one of the best, actually the best, officers I ever served under. I thought the next time I'd see you that you'd have a whole bunch of stars on your shoulders."

Eli grinned. "Well, sometimes life takes a different direction than we expect, but…" he shrugged. "So, how's Laramie treatin' you, O'Rourke, still tryin' to drink it dry?"

The sergeant grinned. "Oh, that'll never happen, Colonel. They shipped most o' the Irish out durin' the war, I been havin' to drink it all muh own self." He laughed.

Eli looked at the captain and asked, "Mind if I borrow this sack o' trouble for a while, Captain?"

The captain scowled, looked from Eli to O'Rourke and shook his head. "Just don't forget where you belong, Sergeant," he growled and turned away to go for some of the promised coffee and biscuits. The two old friends enjoyed the time of reminiscing, swapping tales and sharing stories and the first sergeant finally stood, shook Eli's hand, and said, "We'll talk more when we get to the post, if'n that be alright, Colonel?"

"I'll count on it, Sergeant."

THE COLD SNAP BROKE, and the sun shone bright as the wagons, with Army escort, pulled away from the trees and set their course to Fort Laramie. It was another day and a half before they came in sight of the many adobe and stone structures of the fort. When they approached the compound, the captain directed Eli to take the wagons to the pasture northeast and beyond the post, a sizable piece of land with good grass near the water and the trees that lined the riverbank. The Laramie River made a deep bend to the south, swung back north and a sharp bend back to the south before making a dog-leg bend to give the fort a peninsula bordered on the east and west before the river pointed itself to the east to join with the North Platte. It was the west-to-east straight stretch of the river that bordered the big pasture on the south edge. "You're free to make your camp just about any way you'd like. That village on the far side of the river is a band of Northern Arapaho, they're friendly, mostly. You might wake up one morning and find a village of Crow as your neighbors. I'm told they come in about this time of year. There's a couple cabins set back in the trees there that were built and left by other settlers that camped during winter's past, you can use them if you like, it's always been first come, first served."

Eli looked at Carl and suggested, "Since y'all have wagons, how 'bout I take one of the cabins, and dependin' on what your sister and Charlie do, they might want the other'n."

Carl grinned, looked back toward the wagons and saw his sister sitting astride her buckskin, next to Charlie and his buckskin. "They do make a pair, don't they?"

Eli chuckled. "Never thought I'd see the day, but I

saw the two of 'em talkin' to the parson. It appears to be gettin' serious. Don't know what Charlie's gonna be doin' to make a living and support a family, but I guess they'll figure that out."

Carl chuckled. "Won't be a problem, Meaghan has more money than she knows what to do with."

Eli frowned. "What?"

"Guess she hasn't told Charlie yet. Her first husband was well invested in railroads, he died in an accident and left her well fixed."

"You don't say, and he doesn't know that yet?"

"Don't reckon. "And it's not your place or mine to tell him," cautioned Carl, looking from under a heavy brow at Eli.

CHAPTER 35

LODGES

As the people began making their camp, Eli went to the cabin, looked it over and was surprised to see it as a well-built cabin, one room, a loft, a sound roof, good fireplace, a couple of windows, shelves and a counter. It was more than he needed, but winter was coming on fast and sleeping outside was not enticing. He stepped outside, looked around, saw the wagons shuffling and moving about, making the placement of each wagon beneficial to others. He noticed one family with a passel of kids and frowned as he watched. He moved closer and offered to help, but the big lumberjack looking man with his full face of red whiskers, tufts of hair protruding from his floppy hat, more showing from his linsey-Woolsey shirt that strained over his barrel chest, and hearty laugh, said, "Ah, we got it figgered out. Thankee anyway."

"You've got a passel of young'uns, where they all gonna sleep?"

"Ah, they's usually under the vagon, whenever we can get 'em to settle down."

Eli looked at the sky and round about. "With winter comin'?"

"They gots varm blankets," answered the man known as Arne Petersen. "We come from the northland. We know winter."

"Not like the winter here. Your kids try to sleep out here, they won't wake up." He glanced to the cabin, shook his head. "Come with me," he muttered and started to the cabin. He pushed open the door, motioned Arne and his wife Inga inside, paused to let them look around. "I want you to take the cabin, if you need the extra room, then use your wagon, but don't have those youngsters sleeping on the ground, they might get froze to it."

Arne looked at his wife who was smiling broadly and nodding her head. Arne looked back to Eli, extended his meaty palm, and said, "Jah, we will do that, and we be thanking you."

"That's quite alright, this was too big for just me."

"But vhat vill you do?"

"Oh, I might trade with the Indians, get me a hide lodge. They're almighty comfortable and you sleep right by the fire." He grinned, shook Arne's hand and left them alone to make the cabin into a home.

He stepped back aboard Rusty and turned him back to the fort, Grey following close behind. He rode to the Post Traders store, slapped the reins around the hitch rail and did the same with the lead of Grey, and stepped into the dim interior. He was assaulted by all the smells of the store, leather goods, barrels of pickles, spilled whiskey, unwashed bodies, and more. It was the stench of civilization, even in this remote outpost. He stepped to the counter, loosely called the bar, several wide rough planks that lay on two big barrels and was greeted by the post trader. "Howdy friend, what can I do you fer?"

"Well, once I decide where I'm gonna bunk, I'll be needin' some supplies. But for right now, I could use some information. I came in with the wagon train, and they're settlin' into winter here, and I was thinkin' I'd like to get me a tipi. Would you have one to trade or know of where I can get me one?"

The portly man with a ring of hair that lay above his ears but not on top of the shiny dome, leaned on the counter, rubbed his chin as he gave it some thought. "You know, I don't have one, haven't ever taken one in trade, they're too big. But I heard about one, there's this old woman, lost her man in a buffalo hunt, she's all alone, but she's got herself a fine lodge, yessiree. Now, she's over yonder in the Arapaho camp, name of, uh, *heehtese'eit,* Bald Eagle. Just ask anyone over there, they all know her and know her well. She can be a bit cantankerous, but she might work you a deal."

Eli nodded, thanked the man and went to Rusty, mounted up and started for the Arapaho village across the river. The Laramie River was shallow, no more than a foot deep, and the bottom gravelly, making crossing easy. When Eli rode up on the sandbar, he stopped, Grey came alongside, and Eli looked around and started into the village. Several of the people stopped, stared, the children running alongside until he entered the central compound. When a man who was obviously one of their chiefs rose from his lounging on a willow backrest, and stood before Eli with a stoic expression, Eli reined up and with his right hand lifted, palm open in the common sign for peace, he greeted the chief with "Ya-te-ey. I come in peace. I am Elijah McCain from the wagon train yonder. I am told you have a woman by the name of Bald Eagle."

The chief gave a slight nod, but his stoic expression turned to one of scowling, his forehead wrinkling.

Eli continued. "I would like to trade for a hide lodge or find a lodge to use for the winter. I am alone, and the winter promises to be cold. I could use a warm lodge, a woman to cook for me." He paused, lifted his hand again and added, "But not to warm my blankets." He grinned as the chief slowly nodded his head and fought to keep from grinning as well.

The chief looked about, saw a youngster and barked a command and Eli recognized the name *heehtese'eit*. The boy scurried off, and Eli noticed several of the people gathering about, arms folded across their chests and frowns painting their faces. He knew some were just curious, but others were a bit protective of one of their own. He knew the natives had a lot of respect for their elders and there were times that even the older women would sit in council and give opinions.

The youngster called out, and everyone looked to see the young man holding the hand of a white-haired woman, who was a big woman, not just in girth, but in height. Her long white hair hung in braids over her shoulders, and Eli guessed her to be in her upper fifties, maybe even sixty. But her face, although wrinkled, did not show age, nor did her eyes that sparkled and danced all the while. She fussed at the youngster, who slowed his pace and quit pulling on her arm. When she stood before the chief, he explained to the woman what this white man was asking. She frowned, turned to look at Eli and walked close. She motioned for him to step down and began to touch and pinch, examining him as if he was something she was going to trade for or purchase. All the while as she walked around him, she mumbled, frowning. Turned to look at the horse and examined him in much the same way. When she finished, she looked at the chief, gave a brief nod, and turned back to Eli. "You make meat, I cook! My lodge there!" She pointed to the far edge of the village. "Come!" she ordered and started away.

Eli chuckled, looked at the chief, and saw him grinning and trying not to laugh. Eli shook his head and followed the old woman through the village, as many people began talking and gesturing, most grinning and laughing. When they stopped before a lodge, Bald Eagle pointed to the entry, nodded, and Eli stepped inside. It was a fine lodge, larger than many, with a base diameter of about fifteen feet. The lining was staked down and rose about five feet up the inside. It was to allow air to come in from underneath the outside hides, move up and out the flaps up top. This provided a good draft for the smoke to rise and not fill the lodge and also made the interior much warmer. Several buffalo hides and blankets lay about but were in an orderly arrangement, herbs and other plants hung from above, drying for use later, some as medicines, others as food. Eli nodded, pleased, this was a well-built and orderly lodge and would be a comfortable abode for the winter.

The woman had stepped inside behind him and spoke in English. "Are you a good hunter?"

"I do alright," answered Eli. "Are you a good cook?"

"I do alright," she answered, her face expressionless.

She pointed to the far side and said, "You sleep there, I will be here. You do not cross fire, I split you open!" she scowled and motioned with a knife that mysteriously appeared in her hand at her waist.

Eli grinned. "You do not cross fire either," but made no threat to the woman.

She said, "I be your *Neiwoo*. Grandma."

Eli grinned. "I'd like that." He looked down at the woman, smiled and said, "I go to the trader, do you need anything? Salt, sugar, anything?"

She shook her head no and added, "I put things there." She pointed to an empty area on the north side of the lodge.

"Good," answered Eli. "I'll bring them inside."

Bald Eagle shook her head. "I do."

"No, the packs are too heavy for you. I will bring them in, you can put them where you will."

She nodded, opened the flap, and waited for him to leave.

He began carrying in the packs, panniers, parfleche and set them down near the entry. He knew she would want to know what he had and what she could make use of, both food, staples, and gear. He was outside getting the second pannier when he heard her squeal and clap her hands. He stepped inside, saw her handling the dutch oven, and knew that was what had given her special joy. He looked at her and said, "That is yours. It is my gift to you."

Her eyes flared, and she smiled, nodding, and said, "I will cook something good for you in this."

Eli nodded his thanks and finished bringing in the packsaddle and blankets. He looked around, pleased, and went outside, mounted up, and started back to the traders. As he rode, he thought about the arrangement he made with the Arapaho. He was pleased because he knew that when a woman had no man to provide for her, the villagers would usually provide and protect her until she remarried or crossed over. Sometimes, when the winter was hard and supplies few, the old would voluntarily leave the village and go off alone to die so as not to be a burden. That would not happen to Bald Eagle, at least not this winter. He smiled at the thought, wondering what others might think, but not having a care about anyone's opinion. This was his opportunity to be of help to someone who needed it, and he would also benefit, so why not?

CHAPTER 36

TOGETHER

E li wanted to check on the people of the wagons and turned Rusty toward their campsite. He had left Grey at the lodge and now headed to the cabins, he would see Charlie first and then the others. Tethered outside the cabin were Charlie's buckskin, Meaghan's buckskin, and a strawberry roan that Eli recognized as the parson's. Eli chuckled as he reined up and stepped down. He went to the door, knocked and pushed it open and called, "Hey, got room for one more!" Charlie, Meaghan, and the parson were seated at the table, an open Bible before them and they all looked at Eli, expectantly. "I let the Petersen's have my cabin, so I thought I might bunk in here with you for the winter, what say?" asked Eli, doing his best to keep a straight face. Charlie looked at him wide-eyed and even leaned back as if he had been struck, and began to stammer and stutter, "Uh, uh, ah, uh, we, well we're—" And he was interrupted by Eli laughing, shaking his head.

"So, what'chu doin'? Plannin' a wedding?" he asked, pulling up the last chair to join them at the table.

Parson Shadrach Spencer looked at Eli. "We was just gettin' set to talk about that." Grinned the parson, glancing from Eli to Charlie and Meaghan. "But what we was goin' to talk about, might be good for you to hear too." He turned back to the couple. "Now, the Bible says in II Corinthians 6:14 that we are not to be *unequally yoked together with unbelievers*." He looked at Charlie and asked, "So let me ask you, Charlie. If you were to die today, where will you spend eternity?"

Charlie let a slow grin split his face. "Why Heaven, of course, Parson."

"And how do you know that?"

Charlie looked at Eli and answered, "Because I accepted His gift of eternal life and was saved from the penalty of my sins." He looked at Eli again and asked, "Ain't that right, Eli."

Eli grinned and nodded. "Yup."

The parson turned to Meaghan. "And what about you, young lady?"

"I did the same thing while I still lived at home with my family. We had gone to church one Sunday, and the preacher invited all who wanted to make sure of Heaven to come forward and we prayed together to receive Christ as our Saviour."

The parson smiled broadly, leaned back, and looked from one to the other. "That's wonderful, and that's the best news I've had all day." He turned to Eli and asked, "What about you?"

"Oh, I done that a long time ago, parson. Yessir, no doubt about it."

The parson nodded, then soberly he looked back to Eli. "And what's this about you wanting to bunk with this couple after they're wed?"

Eli laughed. "Ah, just kiddin', Parson. I got me a squaw over yonder in the Arapaho village. I'll be bunkin' in her lodge for the winter."

The parson spit and sputtered, "You can't do that! That's, that's, sinful!"

Eli chuckled. "You wouldn't think so if you saw her. She's a *fine* specimen of a woman, good cook too! They all call her *Neiwoo*. She's a very special woman, yessir. And all I gotta do is bring in some fresh meat ever now an' then."

The parson continued to fuss and bluster, shaking his head and began. "How can you, a believer in the Bible and the things of God do such a dastardly thing and cause that woman to sin like that?"

"Sin? What sin? They don't see that as sin?" Chuckled Eli, causing more consternation to rise in the parson.

Charlie tapped the parson on the shoulder. "Parson, *Neiwoo* in the Arapaho tongue, means Grandma. I'm guessing if you saw her, she'd be about this wide"—he held his hands to his side—"and has grey or white hair and very few teeth. It's the custom of most of the native people for an unattached man to move in with a widow woman and take care of her by providing her with meat through the winter, and she returns the favor by cooking." Charlie grinned, shook his head, and looked at his friend and back to the parson.

————

EVERYONE from the wagon train had gathered before the cabin, and the parson had some folks make an arbor for the couple to stand beneath. Charlie stood on the right, Meaghan on the left and the parson, having completed his message about the importance and significance of marriage, turned to the couple and said, "You may now join hands." He looked at Meaghan. "Now Meaghan, repeat after me. I Meaghan..."

And he began with the traditional vows that included, *to love and to cherish and to obey, till death do us part, according to God's holy ordinance, and thereto I pledge thee my troth.* She repeated the vows, smiling and with tears in her eyes, and the parson turned to Charlie, repeated the vows and at the conclusion... "I now pronounce thee husband and wife. You may now kiss the bride." They turned to one another, smiling, and Charlie wrapped her in his arms, and they kissed long and passionately to the applause of the crowd.

Carl and Elaine had organized a dinner with everyone contributing, and the festive spirit prevailed through the afternoon. As dusk approached, Charlie and Meaghan took their leave and disappeared into the cabin, much to the cheers and jeers of the well-wishers. Everyone pitched in for the clean-up and Eli, after helping a while, stepped aboard Rusty and returned to the post trader. He knew that this was the time of day when the different travelers, scouts, and others would frequent the traders and he was anxious to get any and all information he could about the Bridger Trail. He knew about the trail but did not know it as well as he would like. If he was going to guide the wagons on the trail come spring, he would spend as much time with those that had traveled it, until he knew every bend, climb, drop off, and more about the trail. That was the way of the wilderness, with few or no maps, and if there were any, they were seldom accurate. The only way to really know the trail was to gather all the information possible from those that had traveled the same trail. The Bridger Trail, those words would practically rule his days until spring came and he could take the wagons north, an adventure that he was already looking forward to and had some trepidation about, but that was yet to come.

A Look At: The Trail to Redemption

Plainsman Western Series Book One

A BRAND-NEW CLASSIC WESTERN SERIES FROM BEST-SELLING AUTHOR B.N. RUNDELL.

Every time he squeezed the trigger, somebody died. He thought it was just the way of the war, but after taking a couple bullets and being mustered out, it continued. When he stood over the ashes of his family's farm and stared at their graves, the same bile rose in his throat, and he knew somebody was going to have to pay… and pay with their blood.

This was to be the beginning of a blood hunt that would take Reuben Grundy across four states, pit him against renegade outlaws posing as the Home Guard for the north, the Bushwhackers of Captain Quantrill and the men in butternut and grey, as well as the mighty Pawnee of the plains. His father had taught young Reuben to never look for others to do what needs to be done, even if it means putting his life on the line. And Reuben would do just that, with his training as one of Berdan's Sharpshooters at the outset of the war between the states, and his own time beside his father in the woods, Reuben was destined to become one of the most feared hunters of the plains.

Whether it was for man or beast, when his sights settled on the target, death was sure to follow.

AVAILABLE NOW

ABOUT THE AUTHOR

Born and raised in Colorado into a family of ranchers and cowboys, B.N. Rundell is the youngest of seven sons. Juggling bull riding, skiing, and high school, graduation was a launching pad for a hitch in the Army Paratroopers. After the army, he finished his college education in Springfield, MO, and together with his wife and growing family, entered the ministry as a Baptist preacher.

Together, B.N. and Dawn raised four girls that are now married and have made them proud grandparents. With many years as a successful pastor and educator, he retired from the ministry and followed in the footsteps of his entrepreneurial father and started a successful insurance agency, which is now in the hands of his trusted nephew.

He has also been a successful audiobook narrator and has recorded many books for several award-winning authors. Now realizing his life-long dream, B.N. has turned his efforts to writing a variety of books—from children's picture books and young adult adventure books, to the historical fiction and western genres, which are his first loves.

Made in the USA
Columbia, SC
21 December 2023